Witch Baby and me on stage

Praise for the Witch Baby series:

'Enjoyable, comical series full of interesting characters.'
Primary Times

'The combination of quirky humour, sibling rivalry and real-life problems . . . had me captivated from start to finish'
Waterstone's Books Quarterly

'*Witch Baby and Me* is what I have come to expect from a Debi Gliori book, jammed with hilarious and often gross jokes. I giggled all the way through . . . I can't recommend this story highly enough for lovers of magic, humour or even books. A wicked triumph'
Eoin Colfer

Also by Debi Gliori

PURE DEAD MAGIC

PURE DEAD WICKED

PURE DEAD BRILLIANT

DEEP TROUBLE

DEEP WATER

DEEP FEAR

WITCH BABY AND ME

WITCH BABY AND ME AT SCHOOL

WITCH BABY AND ME AFTER DARK

Witch baby and me on stage

Debi Gliori

CORGI BOOKS

WITCH BABY AND ME ON STAGE
A CORGI BOOK 978 0 552 55679 8

Published in Great Britain by Corgi Books,
an imprint of Random House Children's Books
A Random House Group Company

This edition published 2010

3 5 7 9 10 8 6 4

The Random House Group Limited supports The Forest Stewardship Council (FSC®), the
leading international forest certification organisation. Our books carrying the FSC label are
printed on FSC® certified paper. FSC is the only forest certification scheme endorsed by the
leading environmental organisations, including Greenpeace. Our paper procurement policy
can be found at www.randomhouse.co.uk/environment

found at www.randomhouse.co.uk/environment.

Set in Adobe Garamond Pro 14/19.5pt by Falcon Oast Graphic Art Ltd.

Book design by Clair Lansley.

Corgi Books are published by Random House Children's Books,
61–63 Uxbridge Road, London W5 5SA

www.**kidsatrandomhouse**.co.uk
www.**randomhouse**.co.uk

Addresses for companies within The Random House Group Limited
can be found at: www.randomhouse.co.uk/offices.htm

THE RANDOM HOUSE GROUP Limited Reg. No. 954009

A CIP catalogue record for this book is available from the British Library.

Printed and bound by CPI Group (UK) Ltd, Croydon, CR0 4YY

CONTENTS

For Sisters;
of Hiss, real, imaginary, step, half and in-law
but especially for S and K-R;
this one is for you

A MOST UNWELCOME GIFT

Midnight at Arkon House, and all is quiet and dark. In their attic bedrooms, the **Sisters of HiSS**are fast asleep. This means they won't be casting any spells right now. This is A Good Thing, because just outside their rooms, toddling along the moonlit attic corridor, is a very small girl who shouldn't be there at all. She is wearing a nappy and pyjamas with daisies printed—

Hang on a minute. No . . . NO . . . NO WAY. *Surely* that isn't **Witch Baby**? What on earth is she *doing*?

As any fool knows, sneaking into a witch's home is insanely dangerous, but Witch Baby shows no fear. Surely, if she knew what lay on the other side of the three bedroom doors, she would be wide-eyed with terror, holding her breath – or at the very least creeping around like

a mouse to avoid waking the **Sisters of Hiss** from their wicked slumbers. But no – not Witch Baby. She's not even *tiptoeing*. Toddle, waddle, stamp she goes, until she arrives outside the first bedroom and stops.

At this point a sensible child would turn right round and creep back along the corridor, tiptoe downstairs, then run like the wind out of the front door, not stopping until she was back home, safe in her own bed.

However, Witch Baby is not a sensible child. She's a **WITCH**, for spawn's sake. Not that you could tell by looking at her. Even her parents and her big brother Jack think she is a perfectly normal little girl called Daisy MacRae. But Daisy's big sister Lily knows better. Lily knows that dear little Daisy is actually a **Witch Baby** – but Lily is asleep right now and has no idea that her little witchy sister isn't tucked up in her cot in the room next door. Daisy's been Sneaking Around At Night for the past few weeks, but so far no one has noticed. While everyone is asleep, Daisy has been flying through the dark, spying on the people in her neighbourhood to see if

anyone is as good at spells as she is. She hadn't found even the tiniest glint of magic until now, but here, at Arkon House, the air fairly **fizzes** with it. The closer Witch Baby gets to the **Sisters** of HiSS, the fizzier she feels. Now, standing outside this bedroom, she can hardly wait to find out who or what lies on the other side of the door.

Standing on tiptoe, Witch Baby reaches up for the handle and, very s . . . l . . . o . . . w . . . l . . . y, turns it until she can open the door and peer inside. The room behind the door is a bit of a mess. Actually, the room behind the door looks as if it has recently been struck by a hurricane. Every surface is littered with items of clothing.

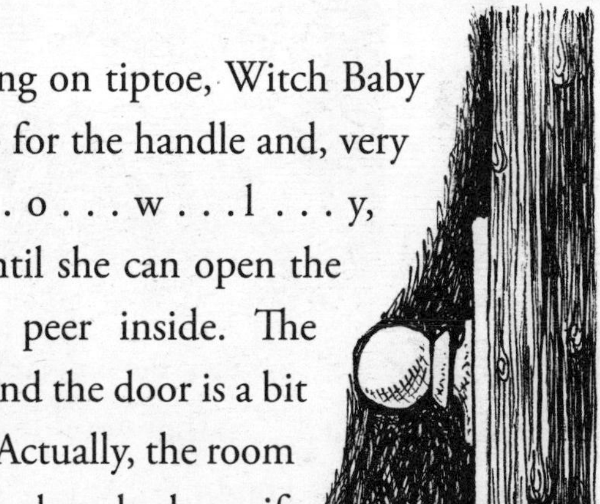

Witch Baby *blinks*. Perhaps the wardrobe exploded . . . That would explain the pants dangling from the lampshade and the vests draped across the top of the curtains.

Witch Baby

pops her thumb in her mouth and strokes her nose. She can hear the sound of breathing. There's someone in this bedroom. In the middle is a tottering pile of frocks and socks and woolly cardigans. The pile is heaving up and down ever so slightly. This is because there's somebody half buried beneath these garments: it's the Nose, the crabbiest and most waspish of the Hisses. Most of the Nose is hidden; only her nose pokes up like a shark's fin, her giant nostrils flapping in the darkness as she sifts and sniffs the night air like a bloodhound.

The Nose is having an awful dream – so awful she makes little whimpering sounds in her sleep, and occasionally her mouth opens wide as if she's about to scream. This is *not* a pretty sight. Oh, dear. Poor Nose. Once again she is having the terrible dream about being turned into a *human being*. **Eughhhh. Horrors.** Being turned into a human is one of the Sisters of Hiss's worst nightmares.*

Actually, all witches would rather gargle with toilet cleaner than be turned into humans. There are two reasons for this:

Reason one: humans can't do magic;

and

Reason two: at least half of all humans have to change babies' nappies.

* Second only to the one about being turned into a dog. As avowed cat-lovers, most witches think dogs are stupid, smelly, panting sacks of festering dog-meat with revolting personal habits and a tendency to cover everything around them in a layer of fur and dog-lick.

No *wonder* the Nose is whimpering.

Before the witch wakes up to find someone staring at her and promptly turns that someone into a pimple,* Witch Baby finally shows some sense. She closes the Nose's bedroom door very quietly and tiptoes away down the corridor. Miraculously she doesn't step on the squeaky floorboard or skid on the threadbare rug, but she does stop outside the next door and repeat the whole exercise. This time the bedroom is tidy, but looks as if a thousand years worth of dust and cobwebs have gathered on every surface. It's the kind of room for which the word 'aaaaaaAAAAAAAA-kerchooo' might have been invented. There, under a moth-eaten cream eiderdown, lies the Chin with her mouth wide open, snoring loudly. Her enormous chin is buried in a fold of the eiderdown, so she actually looks

* Commonly known as an Itch Baby.

quite *sweet* . . . even if she sounds like a warthog with indigestion.

The Chin is dreaming about knitting. She's been doing a lot of knitting recently; not for her Sisters, but for a little girl called Yoshito. In her sleep, the Chin smiles. Dear Yoshito. The poor child really believes that the Chin *is a fairy godmother in disguise.**

Poor Yoshito. She couldn't be more mistaken.

* I can almost hear you gasp, 'Whaaaaat? Does Yoshito's head button up the back? Is she mad? Can't she *see* that the Chin is a wicked old witch?'

To which the answer has to be no. No, no and thrice no. Here's why . . . When Yoshito was born, her mummy died and Hare, her poor daddy, spent the next nine years seesawing between grief at the loss of his wife and joy at the arrival of his daughter. Then, last summer, Miss Chin moved into the neighbourhood and Hare began to change. After nine years of quiet sadness, he now sings in the shower, picks flowers for their kitchen table and smiles more often; but above all, his eyes twinkle and sparkle all the time, but twice as brightly when Miss Chin is near. It is, Yoshito decides, as if somebody has waved a magic wand over her daddy. That somebody can only be Miss Chin. Mischin, the fairy godmother.

The Chin? A fairy godmother? That's like believing the **BIG BAD WOLF** is really Father Christmas. There is, however, a part of the Chin that rather likes the idea of being mistaken for a fairy. For one thing, everybody knows that fairies are far, far prettier than witches; for another, fairy wings don't drop twigs everywhere like witch's broomsticks do.

In her dream, the Chin looks up from knitting a scarf for Yoshito to discover that her hunched shoulders have sprouted a dainty pair of sky-blue wings. She smiles in her sleep and her fingers flutter faster beneath her quilt as she whispers, 'Purl, plain, yarn over, slip next two stitches, turn, purl, plain . . .'

However, don't be fooled by all this mild woolcraft. Even though the Chin quite likes Yoshito, that doesn't mean she likes any other human children. Yoshito is quiet, well behaved and, thankfully, toilet-trained. Just about every other human child that the Chin has met is either noisy, badly behaved, in nappies or a combination of all three. If the Chin were to wake up now and catch sight of a small girl peering round her bedroom door, she'd probably turn her into an *earwig*.

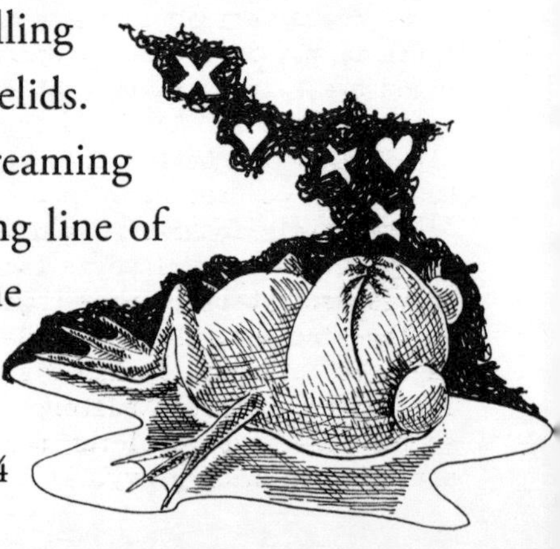

Fortunately she is concentrating so hard on her dream-knitting that she doesn't hear Witch Baby close the bedroom door and wander down the corridor to investigate the last bedroom. This proves to be a small green bathroom with a funny smell and mould growing in the cupboard under the sink. Asleep in a puddle in the bath is the Toad, her great golden eyes swivelling beneath her closed eyelids. Poor Toad. She is dreaming that she is kissing a long line of princes, one after the other – *mwah, mwah, mwah* – and turning each one into a toad, like her.

Ahhhhh, bless. Even though she is a true Sister of Hiss, the Toad has a heart of solid marshmallow.* To the Chin and the Nose's disgust, the Toad appears to love children; especially babies.** The Toad doesn't mind that babies are *Waily*, dribbly, wakeful little **BEASTS**; damp at both ends and frequently caked in

* The Chin's heart is equally soft, but is encased in a brittle shell of prickly thorns, jaggy nettles and bramble stems. Only an utterly determined prince ++ would be able to hack his way through that thicket to reach the Chin's guarded heart. And the Nose? Pffffff. It's by no means certain that she even *has* a heart, but if she does, dynamite might break into it, but you'd need lots and lots and lots. Sadly, it is likely that if she has one, the Nose's heart will be made of stone.

++Fortunately Yoshito's daddy, Hare, is every bit as determined as the best and bravest storybook princes. Against his persistent attacks of loving-kindness, the barricades around the Chin's heart have begun to collapse. To her alarm, the Chin is growing rather *fond* of her tireless suitor.

** The Nose loves children too. Especially oven-roasted and served with onion gravy.

Poo. The Toad would *fill* Arkon House with babies if it weren't for her hard-hearted Sisters. If she were to wake up now and discover Witch Baby standing at her bedroom door, the Toad would be over the moon. Unlike her unobservant Sisters, the Toad would immediately recognize that here was the same little girl she and her Sisters magically transformed into a **Witch Baby** many moons ago.

However, the Toad is several fathoms down, diving deep into her dream, kissing everything as she goes. She is deeply, blissfully, soundly asleep.

Which explains why she doesn't hear when the little girl mutters, '**Needa poo**,' then turns and waddles off down the corridor. Halfway downstairs, Witch Baby stops and frowns mightily. A **prrr-atta-tat-tat** sound comes from her nappy, followed by a rather gruesome squelch. And now there is a very bad smell halfway down the stairs. Witch Baby heaves a huge sigh. So undignified, wearing nappies. Sensibly, she does what any self-respecting Witch Baby would do. She vanishes, leaving the nappy behind as an unwelcome gift for the Hisses.

One:

My sister, tot-killer

Vivaldi was late for school today. She finally arrived at half past nine, apologized to our teacher, Mrs McDonald, handed her a note and slid into the seat beside me, rolling her eyes and whispering, 'I'll tell you later.'

It's not like her to be late, especially today, when we're beginning rehearsals for the spring concert. This year we're having a Noah's Ark theme and the nursery children will dress up as animals. Daisy is going to be . . . the monkey! In the nursery classroom next door, we can hear the littlies learning the song they're going to sing at the concert. Their playleader, Miss McPhee, is picking out the tune on the piano, and high-pitched voices stumble along behind with the words.

Oh, dear. It's hard learning stuff when you're very small, but this particular task is being made ten times more difficult by my little sister Daisy: right now she is being a complete witch. Her voice is very loud, which is how I know that it's *her* belting out the wrong words. Oh, Daisy.

'The animals went in two by two –

Hurrah, hurrah!
The werewolf needed to do a poo,
the spider wanted to do one too,
and they all went into the loo
for to get out of the drain.'

And then Miss McPhee stops playing the piano and says, 'No, Daisy. Now, you know those aren't the right words. Come on, children.

What should we all be singing?' There's a long silence, then Miss McPhee says, 'Right. We'll start with the next verse. I'll help you,' and off they go again.

'The animals went to do a pee –
Hurrah, hurrah!
The spider peed on the bumblebee,
the elephant peed in the monkey's tea—'

'DAISY!' Miss McPhee yells, and then she carries on, this time with the right words,

'And they all went into the ark
for to get out of the rain.'

There are some days when I'm embarrassed to be related to Daisy. This is one of them. I'm blushing to the roots of my hair, and it's not just because of Daisy's love of jokes about **POO**. It's also because Daisy is a **Witch Baby**. That's **Witch**, as in: takes an unhealthy interest in toads, bats and spiders. **Witch**, as in: casts spells. **Witch**, as in . . . **Uh-oh**, next door, the nursery has gone silent. **Huh**? A classful of small children *never* goes quiet.

And now I'm getting a bad feeling. I'm having a Lily MacRae all-systems Code Red aoooga aoooga nee-naw nee-naw panic attack. My stomach is doing back-flips and my heart is hammering, and if I were a cartoon, my eyes would be two spinning spirals and my hair would be standing on end – because this

is exactly how I feel when Daisy is about to do a spell. In this I'm not alone. Beside me, Vivaldi is rolling her eyes and pulling a face. She nods in the direction of the nursery and waggles her eyebrows, as if to say, *What's going on?*

I'll have to find out – I can hear a giggle coming from next door, as if someone very small has just discovered something hilarious. Actually, the giggle is more of a ***cackle*** than a giggle, but only I would be able to tell them apart. It's the sound Witch Babies make when they think they've just cast a particularly clever spell. A spell they're rather proud of. Aaaargh. I find that my left arm has shot up into the air before

I even know what I'm about to say. Somehow I have to find out what's happened to cause the unearthly silence next door.

'Lily?' Mrs McDonald is handing out sheets of paper to everyone.

'Erm . . . can I go to the bathroom?'

'Hurry up then, dear.' Mrs McDonald frowns. 'We're planning the costumes we're going to make for the little ones. We need your help.'

I'm halfway out of the door already, but I'm not going to the bathroom. Instead, I double back, tiptoe past our classroom and creep up to the door of the nursery. *Please*, I beg silently, *let me be imagining things*. Maybe Daisy's ***cackling*** quietly to herself because she thinks her **poo** jokes are hysterical? Maybe I'll look through the porthole in the nursery door, and there she'll be, quietly sitting drawing or . . .

Oh, heck. Oh HELP. Oh, *Daisy*. What *have* you done?

When I burst into the classroom, Daisy is playing with the doll's house; she turns round and beams at me. There's nobody else in the classroom. No teacher. No tots. Just Daisy.

'Lookit, Lil-Lil,' she says. 'Little dollies.'

Aaaargh. I have to make sure that my little sister is Very Gentle Indeed with these *little dollies*.* The little dollies that are waving their tiny arms and legs and opening their even tinier

* The little dollies that are exactly like all the children and the teacher in Daisy's class - except shrunk down to little people who stand no bigger than my thumb.

mouths and yelling something – several somethings – that I can barely hear.

'Help. Help. Save us. EEEEEeeeek. Aaaaargh.'

I may not be able to hear, but I can understand perfectly. I want to scream *Help!* too, but I'm terrified that if I give Daisy a fright, or annoy her, she might accidentally drop, squash, squeeze or break one of the little dollies. And then . . .

Briefly, a newspaper headline flashes across my mind:

KILLER TOT GOES ON NURSERY RAMPAGE!

I close my eyes and give a small moan. Daisy would never deliberately hurt a living thing, but a squashed tot is still a squashed tot, and they send people to prison for that sort of thing, don't they? The idea of Daisy being led away to prison for ever and ever is so awful that I nearly *howl* out loud, but I stop myself in time. I mustn't do *anything* to alarm Daisy – at least *not* when she has her nursery teacher clutched in her fist.

'Ah . . . Daze?'

'Night-night, dollies. Coze eyes. Seepy time.' And Daisy pokes mini-Miss McPhee into a matchbox-sized doll's bed and closes the front of the doll's house. PheeeeYew. I'm just about to breathe a sigh of relief when I see movement out of the corner of my eye. **Aaaaaargggggh**. There are three tiny figures waving frantically at me from a table in the painting corner. As I run across, I see they're stuck fast in the centre of a painting,

their tiny feet trapped in a thick blob of purple paint which is slowly drying all around them. Aware that if I pull too hard, their legs might fall off,* very carefully and slowly I prise the three ailing tots from the clasp of the purple goo, and rinse their legs under the tap before placing them on a paper towel and popping them into the doll's house for safety.

Right. Enough of this. Quick, before someone gets hurt.

'Daisy?'

'MMMmmmmHmmmmm. Not lissnin', Lil-Lil.'

How annoying is that? GRRRRRR. But there's no time to argue with her. I'll have to bribe my witchy sister into behaving properly. Oh, sigh.

'That's a real shame, Daze . . .' I begin. 'Still, that means there'll be all the more for me. If

* *Eughhhhh*. How awful would that be?

you're not listening, then you won't hear me unwrap a square of delicious, melt-in-the-mouth, dribble-down-your-chin—'

'What doon, Lil-Lil?' Suddenly Daisy is all ears. Not only is she now listening, she's almost quivering with anticipation.

'In my bag in the classroom next door are four squares of *butterscotch-chip dark chocolate.*'

Daisy is staring at me, eyes round and mouth slightly open. Behind her, I can see tiny arms and legs emerging from an upstairs window of

the doll's house. *Quick. Not a moment to lose* – before the shrunken tots start flinging themselves out of the windows in a fatal attempt to escape.

'Only exceedingly good and clever Witch Babies are allowed any of my *chocolate*,' I continue, trying not to sound completely desperate. I glimpse the front door of the doll's house shaking, as if several determined tots are trying to push it open. *Hurry UP, Daisy*.

'Wantit *choclit*,' Daisy mutters. 'Wantit *now*.'

She's taken the bait so it's time to reel her in.

'But Daisy, only very *good* and *clever* Witch Babies can have any chocolate. That means Witch Babies who don't do spells at school. That means Witch Babies who turn their friends and teacher back into proper people, not tiny dollies.'

There's a pause while Daisy thinks about this, then:

'Two scares, Lil-Lil.'

Two squares of my chocolate? I've only *got* four. However, I don't have time to argue. Done. Phwoarrrrr, that Witch Baby? Don't mess with *her*. Two squares to the Tot With Attitude.

TWO:

A toast to the nappy

It has been a very wet spring so far, and with all the rain, the outdoor swimming pool at Arkon House is full to the brim. The **Sisters of HiSS** love their swimming pool and can be frequently found *in* it, or floating on *top* of it, or draped *beside* it on sun loungers at all times of year. Even now, in early spring, when the temperatures are Arctic and the wind is nippy, there they are, swimming from one end to the other, sipping as they go.

Sipping? Being witches, the **Sisters of HiSS** can fill their pool with whatever takes their fancy: they've had hot chocolate, vanilla smoothie, pink lemonade and even rocket-strength espresso. However, today's flavour is vintage champagne, and judging by the rosy colour of the Nose's nose and the Chin's flushed cheeks, two of the Sisters of Hiss have already sampled rather a lot of the pool's contents. The Nose **staggers** around the edge and performs a colossal belly-flop into the deep end, submerging the Chin in a tidal wave of displaced champagne. Watching her **hiccuppy**, *giggly* sisters from a lily pad in the shallow end, the Toad **sighs**. It'll end in tears, she suspects.

Shivering, the Chin climbs out of the pool and wraps herself in a long towelling robe before curling up on a sun lounger and sighing happily as she closes her eyes.

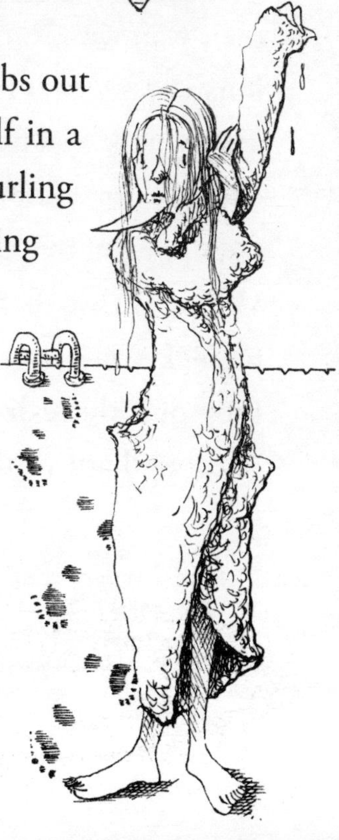

Today the **Sisters of HiSS** are celebrating. Few of us would be overcome with delight to discover a rancid nappy abandoned halfway down our stairs, but the **Sisters of Hiss** are not like us.* On finding Witch Baby's discarded nappy (and its whiffy contents) the Sisters of Hiss were over the moon with happiness.** The nappy without a Witch Baby inside was proof that their little Daughter of Hiss was growing up. The nappy meant that their wait was nearly over. And *what* a long wait it had been. Twenty three months, to be precise. The Sisters of Hiss cast the Witch Baby spell when Daisy was a newborn baby and now she is fast approaching her second birthday. Lacking a **Witch Baby** of their own, the Sisters decided to make one from a human infant. However, they quickly realized that babies, even witchy ones, are hard work. So they left Daisy with her

* Never forget: they may look like two rather odd-looking old ladies with a pet toad, but the Sisters of Hiss are fully paid-up members of an exclusive club that only witches can join. Ordinary humans can try to learn spells, they can attempt to grow chin warts, they might even go so far as to buy broomsticks and dress in black from head to toe, but ordinary humans cannot do magic, no matter how hard they try.

** Weird, huh?

human family until the day when she was toilet-trained and old enough to be taught how to be a proper **Daughter of Hiss**. The Sisters of Hiss have been exceedingly patient, enduring one year and eleven months of watching from a distance; watching *their* Witch Baby being raised by her unsuspecting human parents and waiting till the happy day when she stopped dribbling at both ends and didn't need nappies any more.

'And *then*, dear Sisters,' as the Nose never tired of saying, '*then* we'll swoop in and collect *our* **Witch Baby**, and her real education will begin.'

It has to be said that at this point the Nose looks as if she is about to swoop in and collect a juicy steak and chips rather than a tiny baby girl. In fact, every time the Nose spoke about their plans for Witch Baby's future, she looked

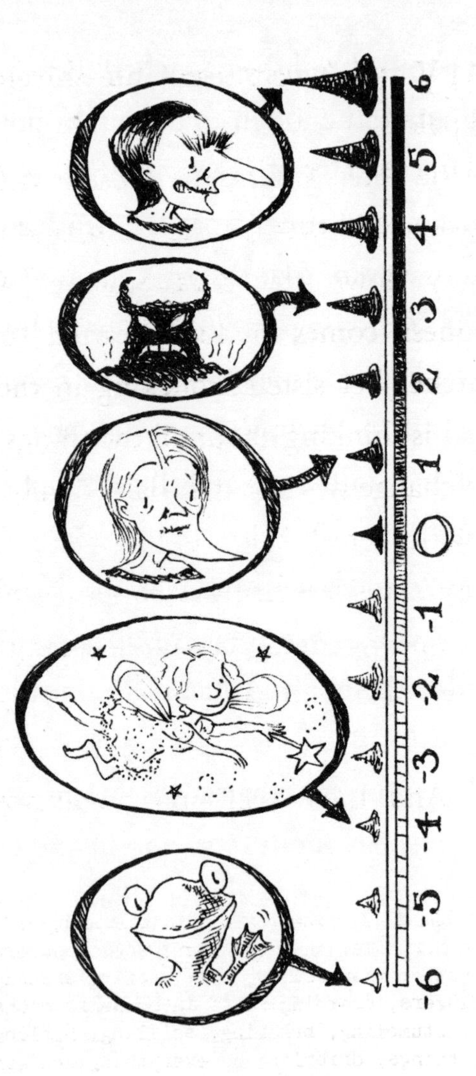
-6
-5
-4
-3
-2
-1
0
1
2
3
4
5
6

so scary and *hungry*, the Chin shivered and turned pale.

Of the three Sisters, the Nose is definitely the Hissiest, followed by the Chin, and then, a long way down the Hiss Scale of Witchy Wickedness, comes the kind-hearted Toad. As she watches her sisters frolicking in the pool, the Toad is thinking about all the things they'll have to change when Witch Baby finally comes to live with them.* So lost in thought is she that she doesn't notice when the Nose hauls herself out of the pool and staggers across to fling herself face-down on a lounger.

'Hey, Toad,' the Nose hiccups, 'when's lunch?' And then, receiving no answer, she

* Much as she is looking forward to welcoming the little girl into her home, the Toad knows that toddlers like nothing better than falling over, poking around with sticky fingers, cramming stuff into their mouths, tripping, stumbling, breaking, spilling, hurling, smashing things, dribbling on everything and generally acting like unstoppable, tiny, one-person disaster units.

demands, 'What *are* you doing, Toad? You look as if you're *miles* away.'

The Toad jumps. She *has* been miles away, mentally building a twenty-metre-high wall all round Arkon House and patrolling it with guard dogs.

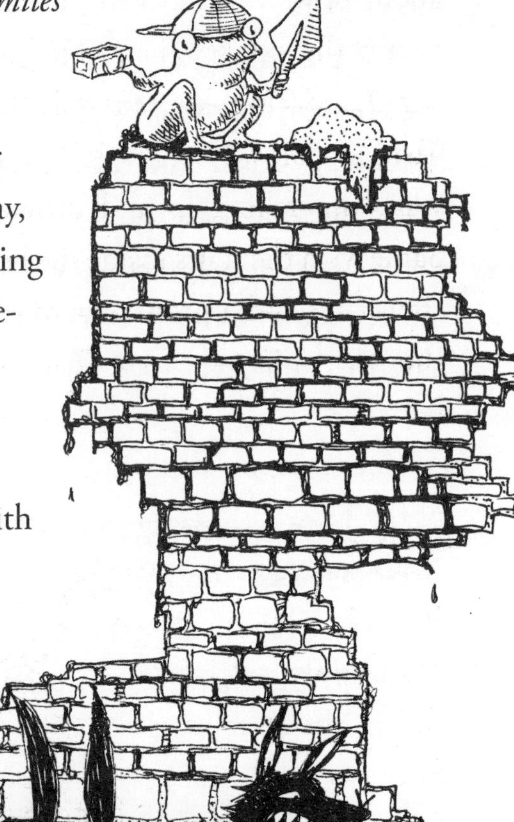

'I . . . ah . . . um . . . I was just thinking about how we'll have to put an . . . um, fence round the pool. When Witch Baby comes to stay . . .' Seeing the Nose's blank expression, the Toad explains, '*You* know. For safety. We don't want her falling in and drow— getting wet. Same with the stairs inside the house. We'll need stair-gates and a proper guard round the fire in the sit . . . sit—' The Toad stops in mid-sentence.

Steam is pouring out of the Nose's nose. And her ears. In fact, the Nose looks as if she is about to **erupt** like a volcano. Seeing this, the Toad backs

away, edging towards the pool.

'You have to be the most addle-pated, pea-brained, nit-witted numpty-headed toad alive,' the Nose begins, her eyes skewering the poor Toad. '*When* will you get it through the wet mush that passes for your brain that we won't be needing gates on the stairs *or* guards round the fire *or* fences round the pool?'

'**We wuh-wah . . . We wuh-wuh–waahhh** . . . ?' the Toad manages, measuring the distance between herself and the safety of the pool. Just in case . . .

'*Wee-wee-wah?*' the Nose mocks. '*Wee wee woo?* Urrrgh. Now you can't even *speak*, you fool of a frog.'

'I'm not a – not a **fruh-fruh-fruh**— Oh, forget it,' the Toad squawks.

'WhatEVER,' the Nose roars. 'You total twerp of a toad, we're not going to be living here once we've got Witch Baby. Soon as she's ready, we'll snatch her and head back to our real home on Ben Screeeiiighe—'

'Ben SCREEEIIIGHE?'* squeak the Toad and the Chin, their voices sounding like twin forks being dragged across a plate.

'Our true home' – the Nose sighs happily – 'where we can get on with the task of *educating* our Witch Baby without any interruptions from humans, stairs, fires or pools. Bit of a shame

* Ben Screeeiiighe is the tallest, remotest, dangerous-est, lethal-est, snowiest mountain in the north-west of Scotland. Historical Hiss-Home since history began, the correct pronunciation sounds exactly like the noise an unlucky hillwalker makes when they fall off a steep bit. Like '*SKREEEEEEEeeeeeeeeeeeEEEEEEee eeeeeeeeeeeeeeeeeeeeeeeeeee!*'

about the pool, but never mind, we'll manage without.'

The Chin and the Toad stare at the Nose in horror.

'**WHAAAAAAT**?' gasps the Chin. 'You *can't* be serious. Ben Screeeiiighe? No trees, no flowers, no shops, no pizza – no, no . . . **NO** . . . **NO**!'

Encouraged by her sister's robust response, the Toad chips in, 'No *way*. I'm not going back to Ben Screeeiiighe.

I'd rather shrivel up and *dry*.'

The Nose glares at her sisters. She cannot believe what they are saying. '**WHAAAAAAAA**?' she shrieks. 'Call yourselves *Hisses*? You two are a disgrace to the name of Hiss. If our poor daddy could only hear you speak, why . . . why, he'd die of shame.'

'He's already dead,' the Chin mutters; 'three hundred and fifty years ago.'

But the Nose isn't listening. Furious at her sisters, she is deaf to reason. 'You two are the Witches of *Wuss*,' she howls, springing up so quickly that her sun lounger flips backwards, hurling both itself and the Nose straight into the pool.

There is a splash, a diabolical scream, and then the Nose leaps straight back out of the pool and runs, howling, towards the open door of Arkon House.

The Chin groans and shakes her head. 'How was I to know she would decide to go back into the pool?'

The Toad creeps to the edge, peers in and winces. **OUCH**. That *had* to have hurt.

'Minestrone?' she guesses.

'Extra hot,' says the Chin. 'I thought I'd save you the bother of making lunch. Dear me. Poor Nose. I imagine she won't be too hungry now.'

Three:

Puppy love

'I couldn't take my eyes off the muffin – it was just hanging there, wobbling around in mid-air next to where Mum was reading the paper,' Vivaldi says, unlatching her garden gate and waiting for me to catch up.

'She didn't *see* it?' I'm not all that surprised. Vivaldi's mum and dad never notice anything.

This is why we decided that WayWoof's invisible puppies should live at Vivaldi's house rather than mine. With a bit of luck, they'll grow up to be invisible dogs without Vivaldi's family being any the wiser. Grown-ups can be *so* unobservant.

'Thank heavens,' Vivaldi replies. 'Not only did she not see it, but Mull was making such a din with his toy tractors that she didn't hear the **chomping** *slobbery* sounds as Boomstek *ate* the muffin.'

Vivaldi is roaring with laughter as she tells me this latest chapter in the continuing story of How to House-train Your Invisible Puppies Without Your Family Noticing.

'And then,' she gasps as another gale of laughter threatens to blow her words away, 'and then – back *up* it came.'

'The muffin?' I'm **horrified**. **Poor** Vivaldi.

Invisible vomiting puppies? How much worse can it get?*

'All over the floor. **DisGUSting**. Honestly, Lil, I had no *idea* how utterly revolting puppies can be.' She stops and smiles fondly. 'Just as well you and I really like animals, eh?'

Since WayWoof, the puppies' invisible mother, lives at my house, I nod in agreement. WayWoof, being an older and more sensible

* Don't answer that.

dog, doesn't steal or regurgitate food very often, but she does smell.*

WayWoof is really Daisy's dog, not mine. Daisy is a witch, and like most witches, she has a witchy pet. The choice of which pet for which witch is interesting because I'm not really sure who chooses who. Did Daisy choose WayWoof or was it the other way round? And if so (WayWoof choosing Daisy), aren't we lucky that WayWoof is such a lovely magical pet?** Apart from her smell, that is.

* How does she smell? And *don't* say, 'With her nose.' Sigh. WayWoof releases occasional stink-clouds which smell of rotten cabbage covered in bad egg and lightly dusted with blue cheese. *Phwoarrrrrrr*. Was that *you*, or WayWoof?

** We might have ended up with a bad-tempered bat, or a depressed dragon, or a rancid rat, or . . . or . . . All I can say is thank *heavens* for WayWoof.

Obviously Daisy can see WayWoof, but the only other people who can are Vivaldi and me. For everyone else she is an invisible dog. Actually, as far as I know, Vivaldi and I are the only two people in the world who are aware that Daisy is a **Witch Baby**. This is because Vivaldi and I were born on the same day under a Blue Moon.*

Jack says the whole Blue Moon thing about having special powers is a load of rubbish. I think he's jealous, but he disagrees, and once he's arm-wrestled me to the floor, he rather breathlessly tells me that Blue Moons only happen when there are two full moons in one month. Nothing special, see, Lily? I wish being a Blue Moonie meant I could beat Jack at arm-wrestling, but then I remind myself that being

* You may know this already, but Blue Moonies are wildly intelligent, hysterically funny, stunningly beautiful, brilliant at sports, musical geniuses, frequently voted Most Popular Pupil at Schoo- Oh, yes, and they can see things that nobody else can. Not all of the above is true except for the last bit.

able to see WayWoof and Vampie and Boomstek is better than using brute force to annoy your sister. So there. Nya-nya nee nyaaaaargh.

Talking of Vampie and Boomstek, here they are, bounding out of Vivaldi's front door to

greet us. Muffin-thieving little beasts they may well be, but they are also the most adorable little bundles of cream fluff I have ever seen. I can't resist. I drop my bag, prop my bagpipes case up against the steps and scoop Vampie up into my arms. Not wanting to be left out, Boomstek puts his paws on my knees and gives a heart-rending howl.

'AWOOOOOOOOO.'

You don't need to be able to speak Dog to know what this means.* Vampie nibbles at my sleeve, gnaws my school tie and licks under my chin in an unbearably tickly fashion. She's warm and wriggly and her paws scrabble at my chest as she tries to climb onto my shoulder.

'Here, let me help. No, Vampie. Down,' Vivaldi says, plucking the puppy off me. Immediately, spotting the vacancy, Boomstek flings himself

* However, just in case your brain is 95% cat, Boomstek has just said, 'O great two-legged goddess with access privileges to the fridge and tin-opener, please, please pick me up and hug me too.'

into my arms and pants in my face. His breath is warm and smells faintly of toast. I hug him tight, burying my face in his velvety coat while he gnaws gently on my fingertips.

I'm having tea at Vivaldi's, then we're going to start practising the music for the concert. I hope Vivaldi's family know that they risk having their windows blown out when I play my bagpipes. Vivaldi is used to the din I make, but I'm not sure that her baby brother, Brahms, will be too impressed. Or the twins, Mull and Skye. Bagpipes are LOUD. When I play my pipes at home, I have to wear ear-plugs. This is why, many years ago, the **Ancient Caledonians** used to send the pipers into battle first. If you deafen your enemies, they'll be too confused to fight properly. However, Vivaldi's family are friends, not foes, so it might be a good idea to practise outside in the garden, rather than in the house. I look up from nuzzling Boomstek to see Vivaldi's mum peering at me.

'You OK, Lily?' she asks, obviously wondering why I am standing on her doorstep, head curled into my chest, making *Ahhh, Boomstek* kind of noises. **Aaaargh**. Boomstek has transferred his attentions from my fingertips to my chin. **Ouch**. Sharp little teeth are testing just how far they can— **OUCH**!

'Lil?' Vivaldi's mum is heading my way, a look of concern on her face. Yikes.

'FINE! I'm fine,' I yelp. 'I think – aieee – I just . . . uh . . . dropped something on the . . . YOW . . . steps . . . Ah.' I squat down and shovel Boomstek-the-chin-chewer back onto the ground, then spring up again. 'Got it,' I lie. 'Sorted. Erm. Thanks for inviting me to tea. Mum says she'll come and pick me up at eight, if that's OK?'

'Er . . . yes?' Vivaldi's mum looks slightly puzzled, but then she blinks and smiles at us. 'I've just taken a batch of really chewy cherry almond cookies out of the oven. I've no idea if they're any good because I sort of made them up as I went along . . .'

Vampie and Boomstek are skidding past me, heading for the kitchen. I hope the cookies haven't been left within reach of them, or they'll be gone before Vivaldi and I get a single crumb.

Vivaldi's mum is blissfully unaware that her baking might be under siege. She jams her hands in her pockets, puts her head to one side and says, 'And what I need now are two brave guinea-pigs to test the cookies for me—'

Vivaldi's halfway across the hall, tearing off her coat as she heads for the kitchen.

'Wait up,' I yell, frisbeeing my hat onto the handlebars of Mull and Skye's twin buggy and following Vivaldi into the cookie-scented kitchen. *Brave guinea-pig?* It's a tough job, but someone's got to do it.

Four:

Total piggery

It's dark when Mum comes to collect me. To my surprise, she's brought Daisy along.

'Hey, squirt. Thought this was way past your bedtime,' I say, peering at the little hunched bundle on the back of Mum's bike.

'Don't,' sighs Mum. 'We've already had a major **shriek**-fest over supper and I wanted a breather before the next one when I tell her it's time for bee-ee-dee.'

'**Not seeping**,' the hunched bundle mutters,

obviously aware that we're discussing her upcoming duvet-with-pillow appointment.

Mum rolls her eyes, apologizes to Vivaldi's mum for not staying for a cup of tea, and in moments we're leaving the lights of Vivaldi's house behind and walking home.

Daisy is silent on the back of Mum's bike, but even her silences are loud. There's something about the hunch of her shoulders and the pout of her lips that makes me nervous. She's **brooding**, and when Daisy does this, it's time to lock the door, pull the curtains tightly shut and hide under the bed. Except we can't. We're at the edge of the woods that lie between Vivaldi's house and ours. The path ahead through the trees is every bit as dark as you'd expect at eight o'clock on a night in late March. Despite having had three helpings of vegetarian chilli plus a huge wedge of treacle tart and home-made ice cream, my stomach is managing to tie itself into a tight little knot of anxiety. *Please, Daisy*, I silently beg her, *no*

spells tonight. No spe—

'**Not needa pee**,' Daisy informs us, adding, 'All dun. Not clever girl.'

Oh dear. In the glow from her front bike-light, I can see Mum's shoulders sag.

'**Not dunna poo**,' Daisy adds cheerfully, the lying toad. At this double whammy of nappy-insult, Mum cracks.

'Oh, Daisy,' she **groans**. 'For heaven's SAKE. Why didn't you ask?'

'Not gotta potty,' Daisy counters. 'Notta potty onna bike. Notta potty inna tees. Notta potty inna Lil-Lil's bagpie. Notta po—'

'All RIGHT, Daze,' Mum snaps. 'We get the message.'

But Daisy's on a roll. All the way home she belts out every single one of the verses she can remember from the song her class is singing at the concert. By the time we reach our garden gate Mum and I are both wishing that the animals, the ark and its vast cargo of poo would sink without trace to the bottom of the deep blue sea.

'The animals went in four by four –
Hurrah, hurrah!
The 'nosserus pood all over the floor,
the effalunt slid innit out of the door,
and they all went into the ark
for to get out of the drain.'

Daisy's still singing upstairs, but at least we made it back home without her doing any magic spells. Pheee-yew. I'm packing my school bag for tomorrow, and on the other side of the kitchen my big brother Jack is loading up a plate with enough food to keep him going through the night. I try not to stare, but it's hard. Jack's appetite is **colossal.** Surely he can't possibly eat that whole plateful without exploding?

You be the judge. On the plate are:

- Four sandwiches which could easily double as footstools.
- One bowl of noodles. (I use the word 'bowl' in the loosest sense. 'Bucket' would be more accurate.)
- One dangerously full mug of hot chocolate with a dense cluster of marshmallows bobbing on top.

- And – to fill in any last little hollows – a tottering column of digestive biscuits cemented together with strawberry jam.

As usual, a faint tss tss sound is coming from Jack's head. Poor Jack. He needs a

soundtrack for everything he does. It's as if he's starring in a film of his life, and needs music to make it real.

COMING SOON:

Jack Makes Another Sandwich

the sequel to Jack's Snack,

starring

Jack Macrae,

best known for his award-winning role in

ATTACK OF THE SCREAMING MUNCHIES

Just then, Daisy appears in the kitchen.

'Naaaanight, Dack,' she says, puckering up for a kiss.

'Mmmwah, Daze,' goes Jack, his jaws working steadily on his second sandwich. Crumbs fall out of his mouth and into Daisy's hair. Daisy blinks, then turns round and thunders back upstairs. Despite the crumbs, Jack is a perfect big brother for a Witch Baby. He never notices anything. Daisy could turn him into a boa constrictor and Jack would just keep on chewing mindlessly, unhinging his jaws to cram more food in, growing steadily more lumpy around the middle, totally oblivious to the fact that his baby sister had just turned him into a snake. This does not make him a perfect brother for me, though. Trying to communicate with someone who stares blankly at you while going tss-tss tssst is really annoying.

'Jack?'

Tsss – tssss tssSSSTT.

'You are a beast. That plateful is disgusting.

You are the beastliest beast I've ever seen. You. Are. A. Pig.'

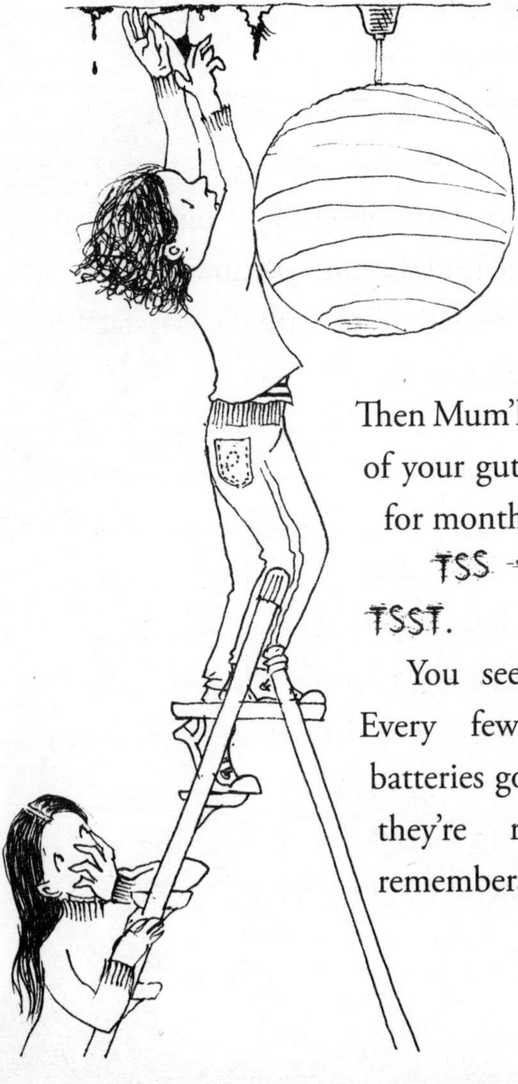

TSS? TSS?

'Put one more mouthful in there and you'll go **BANG**!

Then Mum'll be picking bits of your guts off the ceiling for months.'

TSS tsss TSS tss TSST.

You see my problem? Every few hours Jack's batteries go flat, and while they're recharging, he remembers how to speak.

'Whafff?' he grunts through a mouthful of sandwich. **Eeughhh**. *Don't look, Lily. Don't look. Don't . . .* Oh dear.

Jack has a marshmallow spot-welded to his chin and he's trying to remove it without using his hands. This is not a good look, but I am seriously impressed, all the same. Who would've thought his tongue could stretch so far? Yeeeearrrrghhh.

'I need help, Jack,' I begin.

'Mmfle?' he sprays.

'We're supposed to be making invitations for our spring concert and . . .' I tail off.

Where Jack was sitting is a small pig. It's a dirty pink colour with coarse bristly hairs sprouting out of the top of its head and is making the most hideous *snurkly* **snorky** noises as it roots through Jack's bowl/bucket of noodles. If it didn't happen to have a pair of earbuds draped around its neck, I wouldn't know that this is my brother, horribly altered thanks to . . .

'DAISEEEEE?' I shriek. 'What have you done? Put him back!'

'Put who back?' Dad asks, ambling into the kitchen, undoing his tie and dropping his jacket over the back of a chair. The Jack-pig ignores him and turns its attention to the tower of digestive biscuits and jam. Crunch, gobble, snurk. Dad ignores the noise and runs his hands affectionately through the bristles on top of the

Jack-pig's head. My mouth falls open. Is he *blind?* Before I can say anything, Dad hauls off his tie, drops it on the table and says, '**Eughhhh**. Traffic was a nightmare. Got stuck behind a tractor, and would it let me past? Sorry I'm late. Any food left?' He smiles and shakes his head at the remains of Jack's little snack and slides into a seat beside me.

Amazing. I used to think that I had the most unobservant parents in the western hemisphere, but sometimes I'm not so sure. Vivaldi says her mum didn't see a muffin floating in the air beside her, nor did she notice when the same muffin reappeared in a pool of puppy sick. But tonight it's my dad who once again wins the Parent In A World Of His Own Contest. Not once has Dad remarked on the fact that his only son has turned into a pig. He really doesn't notice. And as if that wasn't deeply weird enough, neither does Jack. How weird is that? Surely he will look down at his trotters and think, *Gosh, whatever happened to my fingers?* When he tries to put his earbuds back into his ears and finds that there are two huge floppy bits of pink pigskin dangling from either side of his head, won't he realize then that Something Is Amiss?

Nope. Not a flicker. Not so much as a single ripple of unease crosses his little smooth pink forehead. Earbuds are back in ears and he's holding a sandwich in both trotters as he pokes it into his mouth. I can't take any more. I excuse myself and head upstairs to find *She Who Casts Spells* and make her stop.

Five:

Down the toilet

Daisy is sitting up in bed wearing flowery pyjamas and a rather worried expression.

'Not dunna pee, Lil-Lil,' she says before I can get a word out. Poor Daisy. Every time she sees Mum or Dad, she thinks they're about to whisk her off to the bathroom and plonk her on the toilet again. Daisy hates the toilet. She thinks that she's going to fall down the hole, that there's **something** living down there just below the surface of the water; **something** lurking in the darkness, waiting for a small girl to appear. I can understand why she prefers to wear nappies at night rather than waving her bare bottom at the **Thing Down the U-Bend**.

Unfortunately Mum is determined to get Daisy out of nappies before her second birthday, and time is running out. In only two weeks' time we'll be putting candles on a cake and preparing to welcome a tribe of marauding toddlers into our house. Daisy, being a stubborn little squirt, appears to be equally determined to stay in nappies till she's seventeen.* However, Mum's constant questions about the contents of her nappy** are driving Daisy nuts.

* And how embarrassing would that be?

** Daisy's, not Mum's.

Poor Daisy. I can feel her pain. Imagine if the only thing your mum and dad ever said to you was, *Darling, do you need a poo?* Over and over again. *Need a poo? Darling?* You'd probably begin to feel like a walking poo-factory. And, like Daisy, you'd soon become heartily sick of being herded into the bathroom to let the **Thing Down the U-Bend** have another chance at chewing your rear. I'm surprised poor Daisy hasn't turned *all* of us into pigs, not just Jack.

So I don't mention nappies or bathrooms. Instead, I sit on the bed beside her, pick up a pile of picture books and begin to leaf through them.

'Story, Lil-Lil?' she says, leaning up against me.

'No problem, Daze,' I reply. 'Soon as you change Jack back into a boy I'll read you a story.'

‘Three stories,’ she says, patting my knee.

‘One story, Daze. It’s late, I’m tired and it’s past your bedtime.’

‘No wantit one story,’ she insists. ‘Not seepy. Want lots story, want BIG story – WANTIT, WANTIT, WAA—’

Just as she’s about to tip over the edge into toddler meltdown, a patch of shadow in the corner unfolds into a huge black dog which lollops across the bedroom, jumps on Daisy’s bed and licks her face until she collapses in helpless giggles. Thank heavens. Waywoof the peacemaker. Where would we be without you?

With her arms wrapped round WayWoof's neck, Daisy calms down.

I pick up a book and wave it at her. 'Story, Daze?'

She looks at me and slowly puts her thumb in her mouth.

'Turn Jack back into a boy?' I add.

'Dunnit,' she mumbles, hauling her mouth to one side to let the word out. **Crikey**. It was that easy? Last year

Daisy could only do one spell at a time. This used to mean that when WayWoof appeared, I could breathe a sigh of relief because then I'd know there couldn't be any other stray bits of Daisy-magic floating around at the same time. One spell at a time used to be quite enough for a little Witch Baby. That was then. But now . . . now she can keep several spells running at the same time, a bit like a juggler keeping lots of balls in the air at once. Daisy is becoming more of a witch as she grows older. And the more spells she does, the harder it is to keep her magical skills a secret.

I suspect that it would be disastrous for Daisy if any grown-ups found out that she is a **Witch Baby**. At first they wouldn't believe what they were seeing: levitating muffins, brothers turned into pigs, dogs conjured out of thin air . . . Then, when it could no longer be denied that Daisy had *Special Powers*, our lives would be turned upside down. Hundreds of television people would turn up at our front door, all wanting to interview her. Newspaper reporters and photographers would camp round our house, all trying to take photos and ask questions. We'd be late for school, trying to fight our way past the crowds. There'd be helicopters with spotlights flying over our house, trying to see in our windows. It would be horrible. Every single thing our family did would be reported in the papers:

LILY MACRAE,
SISTER OF
WITCH BABY,
BRUSHES TEETH

SHOCK!
HORROR!
JACK MACRAE,
BROTHER OF
WITCH BABY,
GOES *TSS-TSS*

WE RAID
MACRAE
DUSTBIN
WITCH BABY'S
FAMILY NOT
100%
VEGETARIAN

After several weeks of this sort of thing the press would start pestering everyone we knew until someone cracked.

MACRAE
FAMILY
'FRIEND'
TELLS ALL
'I PLAYED WITH
WITCH BABY'
BY NURSERY CLASSMATE

and

WITCH BABY

NOT TOILET-TRAINED

BY THE THING DOWN THE U-BEND

Daisy's world would never be the same again. For the rest of her life she would be some kind of *weird celebrity*. She would never again be allowed to be just Daisy MacRae, my little sister. She'd be Daisy the Witch. People would be fascinated by her, but scared of her too. People would pester her to cast spells for them. From the moment the grown-up world became aware of what Daisy really is, her life – her ordinary life as the youngest member of our family – would be over. I know, it sounds as if I'm exaggerating, but I don't think so. Something tells me it's really important that I keep Daisy's witchiness secret. At least until she's old enough to take care of herself.

'Wantit, piggybook,' she says, pointing to a battered paperback. Good choice. This used to be Jack's when he was small, and then it was mine, and now it's been passed on to Daisy. The pages have all fallen out at least once, and it's been mended with sellotape over and over again, but that just proves that it's a story that's been loved to bits.

Perhaps that's where Daisy got the idea for turning Jack into a pig. **Aaaargh**. I look nervously at the pile of books that have toppled off her bed and fanned out across the floor. In between their pages are enough ideas for magic spells to turn our little corner of Scotland upside down, inside out and totally **topsy-turvy**.*

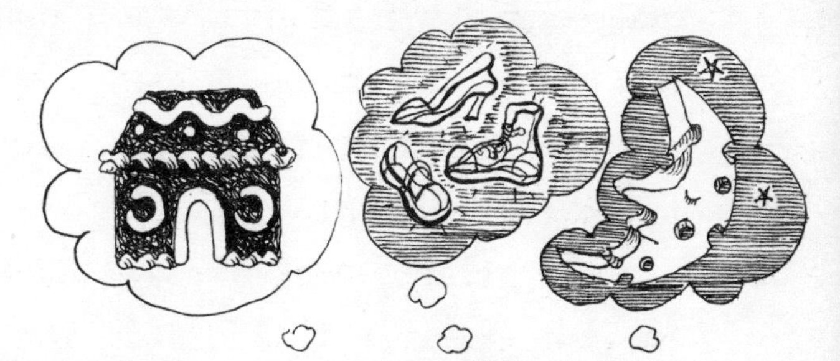

* Not to mention turning our house into gingerbread, our shoes into glass slippers and the moon into green cheese.

Daisy pats my knee again. Actually, it's more of a slap than a pat because she wants her story and she wants it NOW. At her feet, WayWoof stretches, yawns widely and then curls up to go back to sleep. The first wisp of a hideous smell wafts past my nose. Euurrghhh. A story and a stink. What more could a Witch Baby want?

Six:

A bad hair day

After the incident with the hot minestrone in the pool, the Nose's hair started to smell weird. Try as they might, her Sisters were unable to ignore the scraps of mouldering macaroni and putrid peas caught up in her lank ponytail; then finally, when mushrooms started to sprout from the Nose's scalp, the Chin decided that enough was enough. However, she didn't dare suggest that the Nose took a bath and washed the remains of the minestrone out of her hair. *That* would have lead to **stampies** and

shrieKies, because *whose* fault was it that the poor Nose's hair smelled like a putrefying pizza?

Exactly.

Faced with this problem, the Chin racked her brains. How on earth could she persuade the Nose to wash her stinky hair without causing her to throw an epic wobbly? After a few sleepless nights spent trying to come up with an idea, inspiration struck one morning at breakfast.

'Hmmmm . . . but then again, no,' the Chin said to herself, making sure that the Nose was listening. 'No *way*. That's *sooo* wrong. You don't look anything *like* her.' And then, having successfully baited her hook, she settled back in her chair and waited for the Nose to bite.

She didn't have to wait long. The Nose's response was almost immediate.

'*Who* doesn't?' she demanded. '*Who* doesn't look anything like *who*?'

'Pardon me?' the Chin said, making her voice deliberately *vague* and *wispy*. 'Did you say something?'

In contrast to the Chin's woolly queries, the Nose's words stitched through the silence like sharp little needles. 'You *said*, "*You* don't look anything like *her*." I repeat: who is *you* and who is *her*?'

'Oh!' squawked the Chin, giving a *tinkly*

little laugh to annoy the Nose even more. 'Such nonsense. Somebody – Mr Harukashi? No . . . The postman? Don't think so. Ohhhh – could it have been the chap in the pizza shop? I forget . . . *Anyway*, somebody said that they thought you looked exactly like whatshername – oh, you know – that stunningly attractive TV cook, Fenella Thingummy – except I said your hair's too long, but *they* said if you had a haircut you'd look just like her twin.'

The Nose's eyes grew round and wide. 'Fenella Lawless?' she breathed. 'The Queen of Cupcakes? You're kidding! Me? ME? MEEEEEEEEEEEEE?'

The Chin turned aside to hide her smile of delight. *Perfect*. The Nose had taken the bait. Hook, line *and* sinker. Now, all that remained was to book a hairdresser and soon

the stink
of decomposing
minestrone would
be a fading
memory . . .

The next day the Nose and the Chin walk arm in arm towards Klassy Kutz.

'Cut, curl, dye, perm, straighten, highlights?' the hairdresser asks as he whisks a gown around the Nose's neck and seats her in a revolving black leather chair. Not waiting for an answer, he spins the old witch round in a circle and regards her with a critical eye.

'Hmmmm,' he says, putting his head to one side. 'This calls for something biiig and dramatic . . .'

The Nose swallows. Although she's prepared to go through with this in order to look even more like the glamorous Fenella Lawless, she feels very uncomfortable being stared at by this young man. Nobody has ever stared at the Nose for such a long time. Nobody alive, that is. The Nose grits her teeth and endures it. The hairdresser picks up a limp strand of her hair and tssks as if he's disappointed.

'Dear me,' he says sadly. 'Your hair's in a terrible state. When did you last have it cut?'

The Nose wisely decides not to tell the truth – it is quite likely that her last haircut took place before this young man's great-great-grandmother was born. Instead, she mumbles something about being unable to remember.

'Never mind, dear,' the young man says, wheeling the Nose's chair across to a row of sinks. 'We'll soon sort you out. SHAMPOO!'

Before the Nose can say a word, she's being bent backwards over a sink and warm water is sluicing across her scalp.

'Comfy?' the hairdresser asks, rubbing vigorously all over the Nose's head. Bubbles begin to drift out of the sink, and the Nose is surrounded in a warm cloud of flowery perfume. More warm water, more delicious fragrances – and then, as suddenly as it began, the shampooing is over.

The Nose is unfolded from the sink, her head is skilfully wrapped in a warm turban of towelling and she is wheeled across to a wall of mirrors for her haircut.

Across the room, the Chin is immersed in reading a magazine. Sunday, the glossy pages inform her, is Mother's Day. On Sunday, she reads, all mummies get to lie in bed, have breakfast brought to them, receive cards, flowers, chocolate, jewels, paintings, holidays, handbags . . . and all just for being a mummy. The Chin sighs. How lovely that must be, she thinks. Nobody has ever brought

her breakfast in bed or given her a Mother's Day card. Poor Chin. Despite all her spells and wickedness, all she really wants is to be loved. But witches are not easy to love; most people are so scared of them, they'd rather fling themselves off a cliff than give a witch a cuddle. Children have been taught to avoid even talking to strange old ladies with wild hair and funny clothes. In fact, the Chin has gone through her entire life without ever knowing what love is.*

The Chin sighs again. She'll never be a mummy now. Not at four hundred years old. When she was a young witch, she used to dream about having a dear little Witch Baby of her own, a dear little Witch Baby who would grow up calling her 'Mummy'. However, what the Chin hadn't realized was that for every mummy there also had to be a daddy. Sadly, most of the daddies on the Chin's list of possibilities took one look at the Chin's chin, heard her witchy,

* However, there is some hope for her. Hare Harukashi is head-over-heels in love with her. This is utterly remarkable because anyone can see that the Chin is a four-hundred-year-old witch with a chin so sharp you could use it to slice bread. Anyone except Hare and his daughter, Yoshito. The Chin has tried to put them off. She has even told Hare she'll turn him into a maggot if he doesn't stop pursuing her, but Hare pays her no heed. If she turns him into a maggot, Hare will still love the Chin with all his maggoty heart. Such is the way of true love: it is blind, it is insane and it intends to overcome every obstacle in its way.

creaky, quavery voice, or perhaps caught a glint of the magic flickering behind her eyes . . . and that was the last the Chin ever saw of that daddy.

Poor Chin. As the months, years, decades and eventually centuries rolled past, all hope of finding that ideal, elusive Witch Baby daddy faded away. In desperation, the Chin and her Sisters chose a human child to be their adopted Witch Baby. But no matter what they did to her, Daisy would never call any of the Sisters of Hiss 'Mummy'.

Somehow Chinny, Nosy and Toady didn't quite sound the same. Poor Chin. Poor Nose. Poor Toad. Dragging her thoughts back to the present, the Chin lets her gaze fall onto the photo in the magazine in her lap. The photo of a perfect mummy enjoying her Mother's Day breakfast, a tiny child tucked in each arm, flowers artfully strewn across the quilt. A flash of irritation at the smug-cat-who-got-the-cream expression on the mummy's face makes the Chin's fingers twitch, and before she can stop herself, a bristly black beard suddenly appears on the plump pink chin of the no-longer-perfect mummy. The Chin's eyes widen. Did she just do that? The corners of her mouth quiver and she gives a snort of laughter, which she hastily tries to disguise as a **cough**.

'Everything OK over there?' the hairdresser

asks, pausing halfway through the Nose's haircut to smile at the Chin. 'I won't be too much longer. Soon have your mum here looking ten years young—'

There is a squawk, a FLASHHHHHH and a FRIZZZZLE. The hairdresser's scissors fall to the floor with a clatter. Where the hairdresser was stands a large and ugly bird. Casting a terrified glance around, it gives a dismayed honk and vanishes across the room behind a bead curtain. In the sudden silence a telephone begins to ring.

The Chin's mouth falls open. 'Whaaa? What on earth? N-N-NOSE?'

The Nose stands up, drags the gown from round her shoulders and flings it aside. 'Sssserves him right,' she spits. 'Calling me your MOTHER! The pea-brained dodo.'

'You turned him into a dodo?' the Chin wails. 'Oh, Nose. You promised you wouldn't do any magic in public unless strictly necessary. You know it's too dangerous. QUICK – before anyone finds out – put him back.'

'Shan't,' the Nose mutters, stalking across to a mirror to check her reflection. Fortunately she is too blinded by rage to notice when the mirror promptly shatters. She spins on her heel and glares at the Chin. '**Ssstupid**, **ssstupid** and **SSSTUPID**,' she hisses. 'I don't look anything like your mother. Any fool would be able to tell that we are Sisssssters.'

Despite her own promise to avoid using magic unless it was strictly necessary, the Chin decides that this is an all-out emergency and, like it or not, magic will have to be used. Behind her back she makes the sign of the gushy thumb* and blinks – left eye, right eye, left eye, right eye – at her reflection. Immediately the broken mirror ripples as if its jagged glassy surface is made of water, and just as immediately, the Nose's reflection reappears.

* The gushy thumb has been used for generations to keep applause, praise, falsely good reviews and general grovelly, insincere sucking-up gushing forth as if from a tap.

But this is a Nose transformed. Her huge nose is far smaller, her eyes larger, wider and smokier, her bushy eyebrows curved into a haughty arch and her twisty mouth puckered into a plump pink pout.** For good measure the Chin throws in a pyramid of artfully placed cupcakes to remind the Nose of her twin, the glamorous Fenella.

** But only in the mirror, sadly. In reality, the Nose is still as ugly as ever.

'Come on,' the Chin insists. 'Bring the hairdresser back – he's done a great job. Look in the mirror. That haircut has transformed you. You look marvellous.'

'Hmmmm,' the Nose says, twirling this way and that, all the better to admire her reflection.

'Let's go,' urges the Chin. 'The Toad's making a curry for supper tonight and you know you'd hate to be late for that.'

The Nose's eyes widen. Curry? Her nostrils flare. With the Toad's special samosas? Her stomach growls. Would there be coconut rice with a stack of home-made naan bread too? The Nose's mouth waters. All at once she decides to forgive the hairdresser. Poor boy probably needed to wear glasses. Imagine mistaking her for the Chin's mother! **Pffffff** – the very idea! Her fingers flex and flick a spell in the direction of the dodo. There is a small flash, and a cloud of feathers drifts out from behind the bead curtain.

Time to go, the Chin decides, *before the hairdresser puts his foot in it again.* Leaving a small pile of notes and coins behind as payment for the Nose's half-completed haircut, she ushers her Sister out into the street just as it begins to rain.

Seven:

Rain stops play

Rain is still thundering on the roof at morning break time.

Mrs McDonald sighs and scrubs at the steamed-up windows of our classroom. 'Sorry, dears,' she says. 'You'll just get soaked if I let you all go outside now.'

A huge **groan** goes up – this is the third time this week that we've been stuck inside. It's not that being outside in a rainy playground is so brilliant, but being stuck inside means we can't run around or climb on things or make our usual blood-curdling **shrieks** and roars.

'Don't worry,' Mrs McDonald says, heading for the staffroom. 'I'm sure it will brighten up soon. It can't go on raining for ever.'

'Why not?' moans Craig, slumping back in his seat and kicking the leg of his desk. 'Who's gonny stop it, eh?'

'Ah don't care,' says Shane. 'Ah like it when it rains. Puddles and stuff. It's not all that bad.'

'What are you on?' Craig demands, glowering at Shane. 'D'you think you're some kind of duck? Or a fush?'

'Aw, come on,'

Shane tries to reason with him. 'All the rain'll put us in the mood for doing the scenery for the concert.'

'*Oooooh, I'm in the moooood*,' Craig mocks, standing up and grabbing Shane's shoulders.

'*Ooooh, I'm soo in the mood. I looooove rain, oooh—*'

'Shut up,' mutters Shane, a blush spreading up from his collar as Craig waltzes him around the desks going, '*Ooooh, ooooh, rain. Ooooh, oooh, love it – oooh, Shane.*'

Across the classroom, Jamie shakes his head and groans. Another day at the zoo. Beside him, his sister Annabel lifts her nose in the air and says, '**Eughhhh**. I hate it when it rains. Daddy won't let me go out on my pony because ever since he put in the tennis court the paddock always gets flooded . . .'

We all gape at Annabel. Aware that she is suddenly the centre of attention, she carries on, 'It's awful, really. I can't ride my pony when it's wet, and Daddy won't let me have an indoor riding school . . .'

Craig bends forwards and slowly bangs his

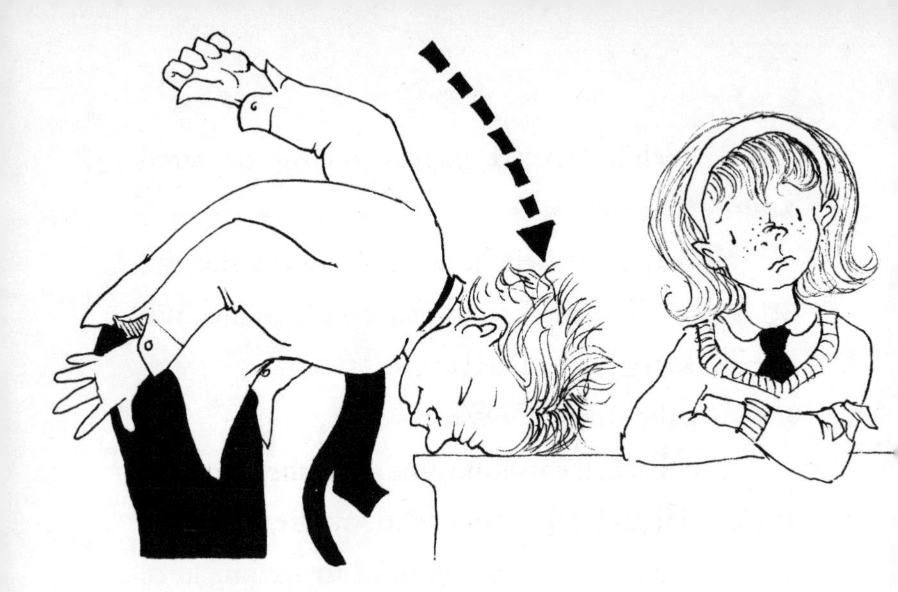

forehead against his desk.

BANG.

Annabel's nose wrinkles, but she's unstoppable. 'It's really not fair – thanks to the rain, I end up losing about a hundred days of riding every year—'

BANG, **BANG**, **BANG** goes Craig's head, and then he stops, stands upright and peers at Annabel as if he's never seen her before. His eyes grow wide and he puts both hands in front of his face as if he's trying to ward something off.

'AAAAAAARGH!' he yells, so loudly that we all jump. 'It's an Annabelly. Oh NoOOOOO. *Help.* Aaagh. Run! HIDE!'

Annabel frowns. 'Whatever are you—?'

'OHHHH, arghhhhh. It's one of the speaking ones. UURGHHHH. They're the worst. One bite and it's fatal. Back, I tell you, get back.'

'I have no idea what you're talking about,' Annabel says, but I cannot be the only one to notice that her eyes are filling up and her voice has developed a slight wobble. Poor Annabel – if only she didn't go on and on and on about how rich her daddy is or how enormous their house is or how many things she owns; if she weren't constantly reminding us how posh her family is, we'd probably really like her. As it is, everyone in our class does a lot of eye-rolling when Annabel starts one of her I'm-so-much-posher-than-the-Queen rants. Oh, sigh.

'Come off it, Craig,' Jamie mutters. 'Leave her alone and pick on someone your own size.'

'That would be hard,' Craig snorts. 'Youse're all dead wee. Ah'm the biggest in this class.'

He's right. When we're all lined up in order of height, Craig is far taller than any of us.

'So that means you're the only one who can reach up to paint the clouds at the top of the scenery,' Jamie says, cleverly steering the subject away from Annabel.

'Aye, so ah am,' Craig says, grabbing a big

brush and tipping paint into a small pail. 'Right. No point in waiting, eh? Ah'm gonny get started.'

'Er . . . I say . . . hang on,' Jamie squawks. 'Don't you think we should sort of . . . er . . . wait? At least till Mrs McDonald comes back from her coffee break?'

'Nup,' says Craig, levering the lid off another tin of paint and peering inside. 'Ochhhh. Yon's all dried up.'

Jamie shrugs and rolls his eyes. At least he tried. Besides, it won't be him who gets into trouble.

'What colour did we decide the sky should be again?' Vivaldi asks, jamming her arms into an old shirt to protect her school clothes.

'Grey,' says Shane.

'Blue,' says Mozart, Vivaldi's little sister.

'Nawwwwww,' groans Craig. 'It's goat to look like it's aboot to rain. It's a story about an ark, no a cruise ship.'

'The sky should be sort of silvery grey and purple. Like a bruise,' says Yoshito.

We all stop and stare at her.

'A bruise?' squeaks Annabel; then, after a second, '*Eauuu*. I see what you mean.

You're absolutely right. The sky does look bruised before a big storm.'

'Brilliant,' says Jamie. 'Well done, Yoshito. I think you'd probably better mix the paint.'

Yoshito beams. She may be one of the smallest in our class, but she has a huge imagination.

'My *fairy godmother* has a shawl that colour,' she says as she starts stirring paint. 'That's where I got the idea.'

Yoshito speaks about her *fairy godmother* as if she's real. If I didn't have a baby sister who is a witch, I'd

probably roll my eyes and sigh when Yoshito talks like that. However, when you're related to somebody as weird as Daisy, you don't bat an eyelid when school friends claim to have *fairies* in the family.

'Hmmmm,' says Vivaldi. She's banging staples into a wooden frame to hold a sheet of canvas in place. 'I'd like to meet your fairy godmother someday.'

'I hope you will,' Yoshito says, giving the paint a final swirl. 'I am sending her an invitation to our concert so perhaps you can meet her then.'

Craig peers down from the top of the stepladder, where he's begun painting clouds. 'Ask your *fairy godmother* to make it stop raining, eh? Ah'm fed up wi' no being able to play football.'

'You can ask her yourself,' Yoshito says, handing the paint up to Craig and adding mischievously, 'But you'll have to believe in *fairies* first, otherwise her spell won't work.'

Craig gives a disbelieving snort, jams his brush into

the pot and applies a dripping *swoosh* of silvery-purple paint across the canvas. 'What a great get-out clause,' he sneers. 'If the spell doesny work, that'll be my fault for not believing hard enough. Ochhhh, what a load of rubbish. *Fairies*? They're about as real as **Santa Claus**.'

'What're youse oan about?' Shane demands. '**Santa** is real. He brought me a mountain bike for Christmas.'

'Oh, for heaven's sake,' Annabel interrupts. 'Everyone knows **Santa's** only your mum and dad.'

'Nup,' Shane insists. 'Ah know there's no way ma mum and dad could afford to buy me a new bike.'

'They probably went out and stole it then,' Annabel offers unhelpfully.

Furious and humiliated, Shane makes a

lunge at her, but instead crashes into Craig's stepladder.

'Watch OUT!' Craig roars, but it's too late. Yoshito's pot of bruise-coloured paint wobbles, bounces and topples off the ladder, then falls to the floor with a sickening **SPLOTTTCHH**. Gobbets of paint fly in all directions. With impeccable timing, this is the exact moment when Mrs McDonald returns from the staffroom.

Eight:

Night watch

It's a long way past midnight but **Witch Baby** is still out and about. While Lily and Jack and Mum and Dad sleep, the youngest member of the MacRae household is **UP TO NO GOOD**. Rain patters on windows and roofs, and so does Daisy. Tonight she is peering though the many, many windows of Mishnish Castle, where

Annabel and Jamie live with their dad and their nanny. It's such a big house for only four people; they all rattle around in it like buttons in a biscuit tin. There are so many floors and wings and rooms and windows that it takes Daisy ages to find that Jamie and Annabel have enormous bedrooms on the second floor.

Jamie's room is dimly lit by a small desk lamp balanced on top of a tottering heap of out-of-date encyclopaedias. Witch Baby tiptoes up to the bunk beds and peers into the lower one. There's something making snuffling sounds, fast asleep on top of the bedcovers, but it's not Jamie. Witch Baby creeps closer. It's a dog, asleep. A very old dog, judging by the grey hairs around

its muzzle and the scent of old dog that surrounds it like a cloud.

This is Petra, Jamie's ancient and much-loved black Labrador. Like WayWoof, Petra isn't really allowed to sleep on her owner's bed, but she does it anyway. Gentle snores from the top bunk suggest that Petra's owner doesn't mind in the least. Like Petra, Jamie is fast asleep. Daisy pads back out into the corridor till she reaches Annabel's bedroom, where the lights are still on. Witch Baby turns herself into a shadow* and slips through the keyhole.

* Handy, eh? Shadows are thin enough to squeeze into just about anything, and in a place like Mishnish Castle they're so common as to be invisible, except in broad daylight.

Annabel's bedroom is like a shrine to ponies. In one corner, beneath a shelf crammed with trophies, medals and cups, all with Annabel's name engraved on them, stands a huge rocking horse, but it's covered in dust as if it's been abandoned. Annabel's bed is a four-poster, with matching covers and curtains printed with horse's heads. An entire wall is devoted to rosettes and certificates, all won by Annabel riding one of her beloved ponies. There are framed photographs of Annabel astride the bad-tempered Polka, her present pony, Patches, her previous pony, Penny, the pony before Patches, and her very first pony, Pookie. In every single photograph except the most recent one, there's a grown-up lady holding the pony's head. This is Annabel and Jamie's mummy, *the Right Honourable Portia Dunlop*, who ran away one day with the young groom who used to look after Annabel's ponies.

Poor Annabel and Jamie. Poor Annabel and Jamie's dad. The castle hasn't really felt like home since the *mistress of Mishnish* left last summer. The children's nanny does her best, but it's not the same. The house is too big, the children are too difficult and Mr Dunlop is always working. As a rule, nannies don't stay very long at Mishnish Castle. This one will probably pack her bags and go quite soon.

Drifting past all these photographs of past ponies and happier days, the shadow heaves a huge sigh. Witch Baby has only been inside Mishnish Castle for a minute, but already she can't wait to leave. She wafts across to where Annabel is sleeping face-down in the centre of her huge bed, and pauses. Annabel's shoulders are quivering, and every so often she gives a little sniff.

Poor Annabel. She's having an unhappy dream; one of the ones that began shortly after her mummy ran away. Witch Baby doesn't know what Annabel is dreaming about; she only knows that the sleeping girl is feeling very sad. So she does the first thing she can think of to make Annabel feel better. She drifts in close, and closer still; then, very gently, she begins to pat Annabel's back with a shadowy hand. It's exactly what Witch Baby's mummy does when Witch Baby is upset, and it works like magic every time. Even when Witch Baby is a little sobbing blob of misery, if her mummy picks her up and pats her back, very soon she feels much better.

And look – under Witch Baby's gentle, shadowy back-patting, Annabel turns her head to one side and smiles in her sleep. Brilliant. Mission accomplished. Once Daisy is absolutely sure she's cheered Annabel up, she floats away,

back through the keyhole, along the corridor and out through an open window into the night. She has one more house to visit and then it'll be time to go home.

Moments later Witch Baby is inside Yoshito Harukashi's house, this time having turned herself into a moth. She flutters around the darkened kitchen, where the table is already laid for breakfast. There's a big chair and a little chair, a big bowl and a little bowl, and a big mug and a little cup. Daisy feels a bit like Goldilocks, gate-crashing the three bears' house, except there are only two places set at this table. In the middle is a small vase of snowdrops next to a little jade statue of a dragon.

When Yoshito wakes up in the morning, she will come downstairs to this warm and welcoming room and have breakfast with her father, just as she has done ever since she learned to walk. Daisy flutters out of the kitchen and up, up, up to the little room at the top of the stairs where Yoshito sleeps in a bed beneath a skylight window full of stars. Every night, before she closes her eyes, Yoshito watches for falling stars streaking across the night sky. When she sees one, she makes a wish. There have been a lot of falling stars this year, and each time she's seen one, Yoshito has whispered,

'Starlight, star bright,
I wish I may, I wish I might
have the wish I wish tonight,'

but her wish hasn't come true yet. Yoshito still wishes on every falling star she sees, but she's beginning to suspect that her secret wish is so big that it will need something more than a star to make it come true. Despite this, when Daisy flutters into the bedroom, Yoshito is smiling in her sleep. Under her pillow is the letter she is going to send to her *fairy godmother*. Yoshito is absolutely sure her *fairy godmother* will make her

wish come true. Maybe tonight, maybe tomorrow or some time very soon, her secret wish will be granted.

Yoshito's breath is warm, reminding Daisy-the-moth that she should go home so that she can be tucked up in bed, as safe and warm and snug as the little girl asleep under her canopy of stars. Minutes later, Daisy flaps into her very own mum and dad's bedroom, turns back into a toddler and clambers under the quilt, squeezing into the gap between her parents.

Seconds later, Daisy's mum wakes up. 'Phwoarrrr, Daiseee,' she groans. 'Not again. Have you—?'

'Not dunna poo,' Daisy lies, burrowing deeper under the quilt.

Then Daisy's dad wakes up. 'Eughhhh.' He tries not to breathe through his nose. 'Oh, Daisy. Was that you?'

'Notta yoo,' mutters Daisy, aware that something horrible appears to have landed in her nappy. 'Notta poo,' she chants cheerfully. 'Dunna yoooo. Notta you, notta doo, notta zoo—'

The bedside light snaps on and Daisy's parents peer blearily at each other.

'Notta GLOO, notta BOOOOO—'

'I did her last night,' Mum says.

'Honey, I did her every night for a week before that,' Dad says.

'Notta ploo, notta gruuuu, notta COOOO.'

'But I'm soooo tired,' Mum groans. 'Please?

Just this once?'

Daisy's dad gives way. He takes a deep breath, throws back the covers and plucks Daisy out of bed. 'C'mon, Smelly,' he says. 'Time to get you out of that horrible nappy.'

'Notta ROO, notta FOOO,' Daisy chants.

'It's a poo, and we're going to the loo,' Dad says through clenched teeth, adding, 'And you need to learn not to do that any more.'

'Notta DOO?' says Daisy sadly.

'Not do a poo, except in the loo,' Dad insists, his voice fading away as he bears Daisy off to the bathroom. Without a second's hesitation, Mum turns over, pummels her pillow into shape, pulls the quilt up to her ears and goes straight back to sleep.

Nine:

No mummies here

Sunday morning at Arkon House, and the Sisters of HiSS are having breakfast. The Toad is unusually glum, the Chin is in a very bad mood, so for once the Nose is the cheeriest of the three.

'Deeeliciousss,' she exclaims, reaching out to help herself to more toast. 'Can there be anything better than a lazy Sunday morning spent eating breakfast and reading the papers?'

'You can't read,' the Chin mutters.

'No, I know I can't,' the Nose sighs. 'But you two can, so perhaps you'll be good enough to read to me, hmmm?' And she crams toast into her mouth and waves a finger at the 'Home and Family' section of the Sunday paper. 'Peeve?'

she begs, her mouth full of mashed toast. 'Reef at foo me?'

'Urrghh,' the Chin groans. 'Speak it, don't leak it. Your table manners are gruesome, Nose.'

The Nose gulps several times, takes a *slurp* of coffee and pushes the paper across to her Sisters. 'Please? Read that to me?'

Reluctantly the Chin picks up the paper, looks at the front page and flinches. Her eyes mist over and she roots around in the pocket of her cardigan for a handkerchief. A picture has just formed in a secret, hidden place at the back of her mind. It's a picture of a birthday party and a picnic and breakfast in bed all rolled into one. There are hugs and kisses, strawberries and heart-shaped biscuits, and a tiny child calling her Mummy. It's a lovely picture, and the Chin would like to savour it, but her sisters are waiting

for her to read the paper, so, with a noticeable wobble to her voice, she begins, '*Things . . . things to do for M-M-Mother's Day.*'

At this, there's a *hiccuppy*, **choking** sound from the other end of the table, followed by a soft **THUD** as the Toad drops to the floor and hops away to the pantry. Closing the door behind her, she slumps against the vegetable rack, her heart and mind full of the perfect Mother's Day she will never enjoy. She will never be a mummy; never – not now that she's a four-hundred-year-old toad. The odds against her ever receiving a Mother's Day anything are as vast as the number of stars in the sky.

At the table, the Nose frowns at the disappearance of the Toad, but then turns to the Chin and says, 'Don't stop. Keep reading . . .'

But the Chin isn't paying attention. The

Chin is staring out of the kitchen window. She could have sworn she just saw a flash of sea-green weaving and flowing in between the trunks of the trees outside – exactly the same colour of sea-green as the wool she used to knit a hat for Yoshito Harukashi last autumn. It was a very beautiful hat, and took the Chin many weeks to complete, and Yoshito was utterly over the moon with joy when she saw it. In fact she was so delighted with her new hat that she flung her arms round the Chin and hugged her tight, which was the first hug the Chin had enjoyed for approximately four hundred yea—

'I'm waiting,' the Nose sighs, picking up another slice of toast and piling marmalade on top of it.

The Chin rolls her eyes and focuses on the newspaper. '*Things to do on Mother's Day*,' she repeats, and then she flings the paper across the table. 'CODSWALLOP!' she snaps. 'I'm not reading that tosh. Who cares about Mother's Day? I'm not a mummy, you're not a mummy and the Toad's not a mummy so there's no point in torturing ourselves imagining the wonderful time all the other mummies are having today. We'll never be mummies, but we will soon have our very own **Witch Baby**. As you never tire of saying, Nose, as soon as Daisy MacRae is toilet-trained, we'll swoop in and remove her from her human family, and then her proper education will really begin – **blah-dee blah-dee blah**.'

'You missed out the bit about taking her

home to Ben Screeeiiighe,' the Nose complains.

'WhatEVER,' snaps the Chin. 'The point I'm making is that there is no point in whinging about Mother's Day right now. We have to be patient and wait till we've got our own Witch Baby; then we'll be able to celebrate Mother's Day.' And with this, the Chin stands up and begins to clear the table.

Pulling a hideous face, the Nose picks up the offending newspaper, tears it into little squares and transfers these to the downstairs cloakroom. There. *Perfect. Things to do on Mother's Day*: turn an upsetting newspaper article into toilet paper for bottom-wiping purposes. Returning from this little act of revenge, the Nose sees the Chin pluck a white envelope off the mat by the front door and tuck it into her pocket.

'Where did that come from?' the Nose demands.

'Where did what come from?' the Chin says, backing away from her Sister.

'That envelope you just picked up,' the Nose insists. 'Come on. I saw you do it.'

'Um. **Yerrrrsss. Oh**! This old thing?' the Chin squeaks, tugging a corner of the envelope back out of her pocket and pretending to study it. '**Pfffff**. It's just a bit of junk mail. Something to do with d-d-double glazing. I'll take it to the paper recycling bin.' She edges towards the foot of the stairs and turns to go.

'How peculiar,' muses the Nose. 'It's Mothering Sunday, isn't it?'

'**Erm**. Yes . . . Why do you ask?' quavers the Chin, not waiting to hear the answer.

'Because there isn't any post on a SUNDAY,' shrieks the Nose as the Chin vanishes upstairs.

'So you're telling a great big porky—'

'Splendid,' interrupts the Toad, appearing at the kitchen door. 'I was wondering what to make for supper tonight. How clever of you, Nose. A great big pork roast sounds perfect. **Mmmmmmm-yum**. With apple sauce, sage and onion mini-muffins and . . .'

Many moments pass as the Nose considers this delicious menu. Her mouth waters at the vision of herself carving a healthy slab of perfectly roasted pork plus crackling, pronging it onto her fork along with half a sage and onion muffin, topping it with a dollop of apple sauce, twirling the lot through a pool of gravy and getting it ready to pop into her open mouth when . . .

'Erm,' the Toad whispers, passing her a clean handkerchief, 'you're, um, **drooling**, Nose.'

Upstairs, in her bedroom, the Chin wedges a chair beneath the door handle to make sure she will not be interrupted. Then she sits on her bed, carefully removes the envelope from her pocket and examines it. There, on the front, is her name, written with ink in a child's best handwriting:

Recognizing the writing, the Chin smiles. This letter is from Yoshito Harukashi; the child who believes the Chin is her fairy godmother. Wondering why the little girl is writing to her on a Sunday, the Chin tears open the envelope and is immediately stunned by what lies inside.

It's a home-made card with three figures drawn on the front. Even the Chin can see what it represents. There is Hare Harukashi, Yoshito's father, smiling a huge red smile nearly as vast as the flower in his buttonhole. Beside him is Yoshito in a pale yellow dress with flowers in her hair, and there is—

The Chin gasps. Were she not already sitting down, she suspects she might have fallen to the floor, so weak and faint does she feel. Her eyes are glued to the card – for there she is, chin out-thrust, a bouquet of flowers in her arms, her hair upswept on top of her head and wearing a long white dress with a lacy train. It would appear that Yoshito has drawn the Chin as a bride at a wedding. A wedding? What on earth is the child thinking of? Holding her breath, the Chin opens the card. Inside, Yoshito has written:

Dear Mischin
Happy Fairy Godmother's Day
Love from Yoshi
P.S. Please, please come to our school concert on Friday with Papa
XXXXXXXXXXXXXXXXXXXXXXXXXXXXX
XXXXXXXXXXXXXX

Despite being a very old and **SCARY** witch, the Chin feels as if she is about to burst into tears. Nobody has ever sent her a card on Mother's Day. Suddenly all kinds of unfamiliar warm and fuzzy feelings threaten to carry her off on a tide of pink bubbles. To her horror, the Chin feels her brain turning into pink marshmallow. She grits her teeth and sticks out her chin. She must not give way. She must remember her destiny; once a ***witch***, always a ***witch***. She is a **Sister of Hiss**, not a *fairy*, not a mummy, and most definitely NOT a bride.

And now she is digging in her pocket to find a handkerchief, because for some reason (why, she has no idea) fat, salty droplets are leaking out of her eyes.

'Bahhhhh, humbug,' she snorts at her red-eyed reflection. 'Pull yourself together. You're a

Sister of HiSS, not a . . . NOT a Mrs of his.' And forcing her mouth into a scowl, she drops Yoshito's card onto her dusty dressing table and heads downstairs to see what the Toad is cooking for supper.

Ten:

Here comes the rain (again)

This morning it's *my* turn to be late for school. *My* turn to roll my eyes at Vivaldi, apologize to Mrs McDonald and hand her a note explaining why I'm late. For once, it's not Daisy's fault, but the weather's. It rained non-stop all weekend, and late last night, water started dripping through Jack's bedroom ceiling. Jack didn't hear a thing because he had his earbuds in and was

fast asleep. By the time he woke up feeling damp and chilly, it was the middle of the night, his desk was awash, his carpet had sprouted puddles and it was obvious that Something Had To Be Done. The Something turned out to be Jack moving into Daisy's room until the roof could be fixed and his room drained, dried and redecorated. Jack moved into Daisy's room, and Daisy, her cot, her magical dog, her toys, her changing mat and ten million tons of her toddler-tat all moved into my bedroom. My small bedroom.

Still, it could be worse. I could, for instance, be Jack. Poor him. All his books are drying out on radiators around the house, his bedroom ceiling has developed so many cracks a huge part of it fell off onto the floor, and his bedroom carpet is ruined, dumped in a heap outside next to the dustbins. By contrast, Daisy's room is lovely and warm and dry, but I can tell that Jack isn't too happy about being surrounded by pink flowery fairy wallpaper and posters of baby rabbits and lambs.

By the time Mum and Dad found buckets and pails to catch the drips, then moved everything out of Jack's room, it was breakfast time, and we only had a few minutes to grab a quick bowl of cereal before setting off to school. Outside it was still pouring, so instead of walking, we all piled into Dad's car and sat with our breath misting up the windows while he tried over and over again to start the engine.

Then we all got out and ran through the rain and squashed into Mum's car. It started immediately, but made a very loud squealing sound when Dad drove round corners.

EEEEeeeEEEEEEEeeeeeEEE-ee-ee-ee.

Daisy thought this was hilarious and squealed back, 'Eeee-Eeeee-Eeee, silly ole car,' until I began to wish Jack had a spare pair of earbuds for me. Then, when we were quite close to Jack's school, Dad groaned and the car began to slow down. In front of us was a long queue of cars, none of them moving.

'What's wrong?' I asked. 'Why have all those cars stopped?'

'EeeEEE-ee? Ee-Eee-EE-ee?' Daisy demanded.

Dad ignored us and pulled over to the side of the road and hauled on the handbrake.

Tss Tsss tssstStsss, went Jack.

Dad flung open his door and got out to investigate what was going on. We waited as rain ran down the windows and the outside world began to vanish in the mist from our breath.

Tss Tsss tsss, went Jack.

'Eeee-EE -eeeEE,' replied Daisy.

I gritted my teeth. It was twenty past nine. I was *really* late now. Everybody would have started without me.

Tsss tsss tsstssss.

'Eee-Eee-eee-EEe-EEEEEEEeeeeee. Not needa baffroom. Not dunna poo.'

The lying wee toad. The inside of the car began to smell horrible, but it was too wet outside to even think about opening any windows.

Jack's nose wrinkled and he removed his earbuds to glare at Daisy. 'Ewwww. Daiseeeeee,'

he gasped. 'That is disGUSting.'

''GUSting,' Daisy agreed cheerfully. 'Notta poo. Dunna ewwww.'

This is shaping up to be one of those days when I wish I could press 'rewind' and find myself back under my bedcovers, instead of sitting in a cold metal box breathing in air that smells like it has been recently exhaled by the Stinky-Cheese Man and his friend, Week-Old-Warm-Prawn Boy.

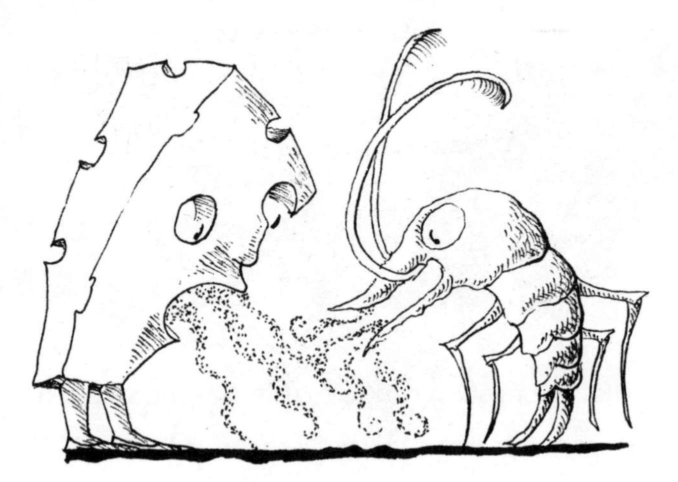

After what felt like centuries had passed, the door opened and Dad climbed back inside. 'The road's flooded up ahead,' he said, turning on the engine. 'We'll have to go the long way round,' then, a second later, 'EUGHHHHHH, Daisy. Was that you?'

This was one of those questions which fortunately didn't really need an answer. Daisy raked Dad with a withering stare and jammed her fingers in her ears.

'Not lissnin', Dada,' she said. 'Lissnin' to moo sick. Lalala LALA la. Tiss TISSTISS. Not hearin'. La la LA. Wot sayin?'

By the time Dad had dropped Jack off at his school, changed Daisy's nappy in the back of the car and finally arrived at our school, we were an hour and a half late. We splashed across the playground, trying to avoid the really deep puddles, before running inside. The cloakroom was full of wellies and raincoats and all the windows had steamed up. I could hear Miss McPhee playing the piano and the little ones practising their song. Soon they'll be singing it for real. On the wall calendar it said:

TODAY IS MONDAY 23RD MARCH

THE WEATHER IS RAINY

Yikes. Only four days to go till the concert? AAAARGHHHHH. There was so much to do before then. Mrs McDonald is putting the finishing touches to Daisy's monkey costume and our whole class is making masks and ears for the little ones' costumes. For the previous month we've all been bringing in boxes and bags of things we thought might come in useful. There are old sheets, ancient velvet curtains and an entire flock of grubby sheepskin rugs. There's a boxful of balls of orange knitting wool and a black plastic bin-bag crammed with scraps of fake fur that smell a bit weird. There's one crate stuffed with rolls of wallpaper and another with hundreds of ping-pong balls layered inside. Jamie's brought in a bag of pheasant feathers, and last week Annabel staggered in with a suitcase crammed with miles of wispy blue silk.

When I walk into class, hardly anyone looks up: they're all working flat out, concentrating hard on getting the costumes completed in time for the concert. Shane and Craig have almost finished their elephant mask. It's really brilliant: a long bendy trunk made out of one leg of a pair of woolly tights stuffed with wadding, and Craig's cutting out the second of a pair of realistically wrinkly ears from a sheet of grey leather.

'These are amazing,' Vivaldi says, picking up the finished ear and stroking it.

'Aye. Dead realistic, eh?' Craig grins.

'Yeah, but you'd better hope your big brother disnae come to the concert, eh no?' Shane mutters, stuffing more wadding down the elephant's trunk and adding, 'He'll mollicate* you if he sees what you've done to his leather jacket.'

Crikey. Let's hope Craig's big brother stays at home grinding his knives on Friday night. If he's bigger than Craig, he must be *enormous*.

Thanks to Yoshito, Annabel is

* Ancient Scottish for murrrderrr.

busy stapling each end of a pile of long strips of blue silk onto thin lengths of wood. When Yoshito saw the blue silk emptied out all over the floor, it gave her the beginning of an idea.

'It's the sea, Annabel. You have brought the sea in your suitcase.'

Annabel's nose wrinkled. 'Don't be silly. It's Mummy's silk that she bought cheap in Hong Kong.'

Yoshito wasn't in the least discouraged by this, and insisted the blue silk would make a perfect sea for the ark to float on. For once Annabel didn't sneer or say something crushing. Instead, she picked up a length of silk and wafted it gently back and forth, frowning as she thought.

'You're absolutely right,' she said, a faint hint of a smile tugging at the corners of her mouth. 'And I've just had an idea for how we can make it work.'

I have to admit it: Annabel's idea is stunning. On the night, the blue silk is going to look exactly like the sea. Vivaldi and I are making the wasp, ant and bumblebee costumes, which means our desks are covered with ping-pong balls and bendy wool-wrapped feelers and legs. We've made giant pom-poms for the bee and wasp bodies, and we're just about to start on the ant's body when the bell rings for lunch. A huge groan goes up from everyone.

'Not yet,' moans Jamie. 'I've still got tons to do before lunch.'

'We'll never get it all finished in time,' Vivaldi sighs, looking down at our pile of carefully cut-out ant segments all lined up and waiting to be painted.

'We're gonny have to come in at night to get it all done,' Shane groans as we head into the hall for lunch. At the far end of the room, behind the tables where the dinner lady dishes out the food, are all our bits of scenery for the play, propped up against the wall. From a distance they look really convincing, just as grey and stormy as the weather outside. Yoshito's second batch of purply-grey paint was even better than the first one that Shane spilled, and Craig made a fantastic job of painting the storm clouds. They look so realistic, I can almost feel the rain dripping on my head.

Uh-oh. I *can* feel the rain.

Drip, drip. There it is again. Drops of cold water are falling off the ceiling and landing on me. Somewhere over our heads, the school roof is leaking. This is *not* good news. In fact, this is such bad news that I decide there and then that it hasn't happened. *What rain? What leak? What drips?* I'm not going to tell anyone that the roof is leaking – because if I do, then we'll probably be sent home till the roof is mended, and that would mean we'd have to cancel the concert. All of a sudden I realize how much we've all been looking forward to our concert – especially the little ones, who have been growing more and more excited, the closer Friday comes.

I look up at the ceiling and cross my fingers tightly behind my back. *Please*, I beg silently. *Don't leak. Please stop dripping.*

'Soup, Lily?' the dinner lady asks. 'LEEK and potato today.'

Eleven:

The Toad takes charge

In the kitchen at Arkon House, the telephone begins to ring.

'Cominggggg,' the Toad carols, dropping her whisk into the bowl of meringue mix she's been beating. She picks up the receiver just as the Nose appears in the kitchen doorway.

'Helloooo?' the Toad says. 'Arkon House. How can I help you?'

The Nose strains to hear but can only make out a distant chittering sound, like the cheeping of far-off birds.

'No,' the Toad sighs. 'But I can give her a message if you like.'

For me? the Nose mimes, but the Toad shakes her head and sketches a vast chin in the air with one webbed foot.

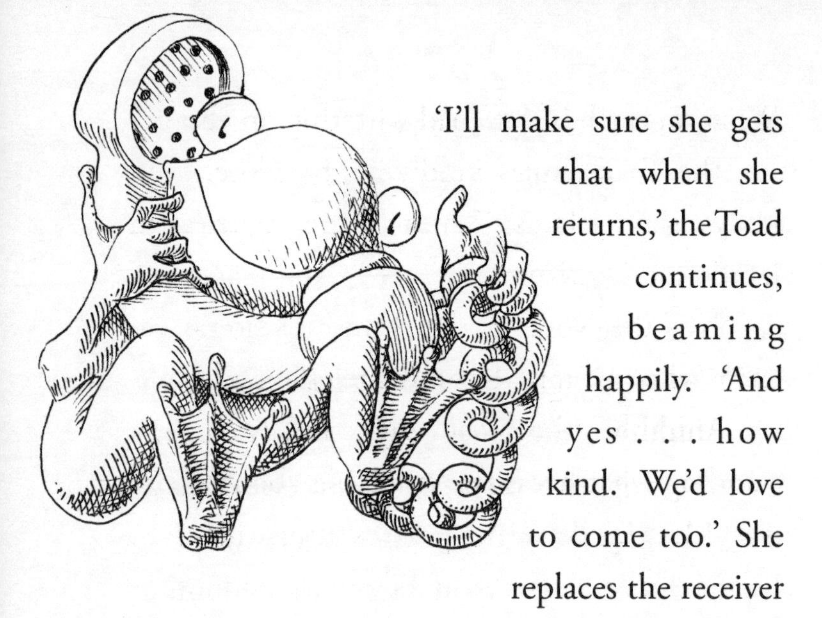

'I'll make sure she gets that when she returns,' the Toad continues, beaming happily. 'And yes . . . how kind. We'd love to come too.' She replaces the receiver and is about to return to her meringue mix, but the Nose has scuttled across the kitchen and is now standing in her way.

'Sssso?' she demands. 'Who was that? Who rang?'

Mind full of cooking thoughts, the Toad shakes her head. 'No, dear. It's a *mirr*-ang, not a *who*-rang.'

The Nose stares at her Sister in puzzlement.

What on earth is the Toad wittering on about?

The Toad smiles kindly at the Nose. 'You know,' she explains. 'I mean a meringue, as in lemon meringue pie.'

'No,' the Nose groans. 'I mean, who rang – as in: who just rang us on the telephone?'

'Ahhhhh,' the Toad says, finally understanding what her Sister is talking about. 'That was Mr Harukashi. It's so exciting! Hoorah, hoorah for Mr Harukashi! Because of him, we're going to get to see our precious little **Witch Baby**. He has invited all of us to his daughter's school concert.'

The Nose frowned. 'All of us?' she sneered. 'ALL of us? I don't think so. *I* can go, and *the Chin* can go – but you, you twit of a toad, if you think for one minute that you can come too, you're living in a *fairytale*.'

'Why NOT?' squawked the Toad. 'Why

can't I go? What's wrong with me coming to the concert? I NEVER get to do ANYTHING. It's always you and the Chin who go out, while I'm left at home, cooking and cleaning and mending like . . . like CINDERELLA.'

There's a *clatter*, a **ger-doink**, then a sproingy, sproingy twonk as the egg-whisk bounces across the kitchen and comes to rest at the Nose's feet.

'Oh, do get a grip, Toad,' snaps the Nose. 'You know exactly why you can't come to the concert: we're trying to disguise the fact that we're witches – yes? While we're forced to live here in order to keep an eye on our **Witch Baby**, we have to pretend to be normal humans just like our neighbours – yes? With me so far? Right – pay attention because I'm not going to say it again – NORMAL HUMANS DO NOT BRING THEIR TALKING TOADS ALONG WITH THEM TO CONCERTS—'

Just then, the kitchen door opens and in comes the Chin. Her hair is plastered to her head and her shoes are making squelching sounds.

'**Eughhhh**,' she groans, kicking off her shoes and sinking into a chair. 'What filthy weather. I'm soaked to the skin.'

The Nose stares at her wet sibling. 'Tssssk. You look like a drowned rat, Sister dear,' she remarks nastily, twirling a strand of her own hair around her finger. 'You'll have to smarten up your appearance because we've been invited to a concert this Friday.'

It's on the tip of the Chin's tongue to say that she's already been invited to a concert on Friday, but she stops herself just in time. If she said that, the Nose would demand to know who had invited her, and when, and then the secret letter from Yoshito would be a secret no longer. Wisely the Chin keeps silent, smiling and nodding at her sister as if to say, *Gosh! A concert! How wonderful!*

'Yerrrs,' the Nose adds. 'It's your admirer,

Hare Harukashi, who invited us. Apparently it's his daughter's school concert.'

The Chin grits her teeth. *I know*, she wants to say. *I know because she invited me. Just me, not you, you foul hag*. Somehow she manages to keep the smile on her face as the Nose continues.

'Thank goodness I had my hair done, but poor old you, Chin – your hair's a mess and you look like an ancient granny.'

'Thanks,' mutters the Chin, standing up and heading for the door.

'You really ought to make more of an effort with your appearance,' the Nose says, grinning like a wolf. 'I cannot imagine why Mr Harukashi likes you so much. You never dress up or wear make-up or—'

'SHUT UP!' the Chin shrieks. 'Read my pale lipstick-free lips. I don't CARE what you think about my appearance. Mr Harukashi likes me perfectly well as a witch, not some kind of dress-up dolly. Witches are supposed to look like me. We're the **Sisters of HiSS**, not the *Frillies of Kiss*. Now, if you'll excuse me, I'm off to squeeze my chin warts.' And with that, she sweeps out of the kitchen. Moments later the Nose and the Toad hear a bedroom door slam upstairs.

'Dear, dear,' the Nose remarks. 'What a grumpy old troll she's turning into. If she's not careful, Mr Harukashi will decide she's too old and ugly and fall in love with somebody else.'*

'**Rubbish**!' yelps the Toad, rising to the Chin's defence. 'You're just jealous. Mr Harukashi loves

* Inside the Nose's head, a little voice cackled, 'Like me, for instance,' and then the same little voice added waspishly, 'Not that I care one jot for that silly little man but . . . if he fell in love with wonderful, beautiful MEEEE, it would annoy the pantaloons off my grumpy troll of a Sister.'

our Sister, and nothing and nobody will change that.'

'I am so not jealous,' the Nose lies, adding, 'ANYWAY, she doesn't love him. And she never will, so there. Nya-nya . . .'

But the Toad isn't listening any more. She's suddenly had an idea that is so wonderful, so *fluffy* and *pink* and *perfect*, that she can barely stop herself from laughing out loud and dancing round the kitchen. Her head is filling up with bubbles, her chest is full of warm flower-scented air and she feels as if any second she might float right up off the ground and be carried up to the ceiling on a tide of white lacy froth.

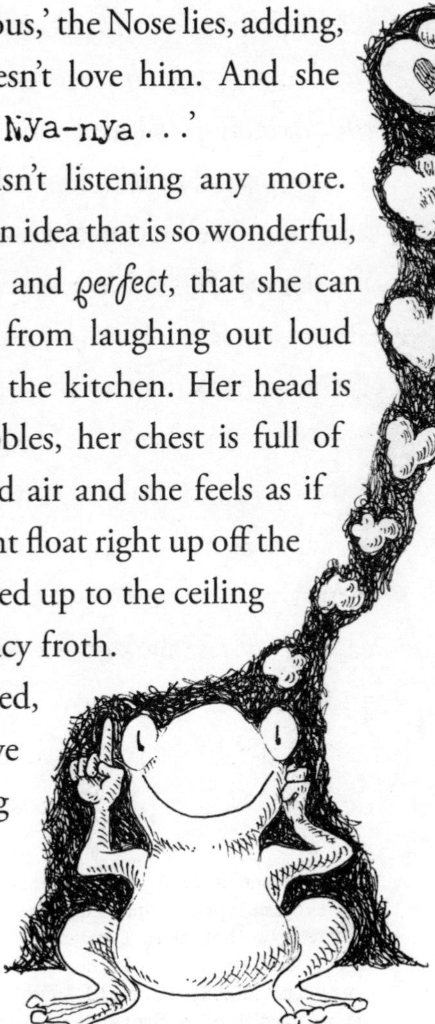

What is needed, she realizes, is a love potion. Something to make the Chin fall head over heels in love with Hare Harukashi. *And then*, she thinks, hugging herself with delight, *then we can have a wedding, and that means I'll get to be a bridesmaid, just like I've always, always wanted.* The Toad's eyes soften into toffee-coloured pools of bliss. It is, she decides, one of the best ideas she's ever had. It is utterly, totally—

The Toad blinks and drags herself back to the present. From across the kitchen, the Nose is giving her a very searching stare. The Toad **gulps**. *Careful*, she tells herself. *Making a love potion is a brilliant idea, but it mustn't fall into the wrong hands.*

Or, she adds, *down the w r o n g throat . . .*

'I think I'll start making supper,' she says, knowing that the Nose will immediately find something else to do rather than offer to help with the cooking. Sure enough, the Nose's eyes swivel wildly and she starts looking very uncomfortable. *Perfect*, the Toad thinks. *Soon she'll be off, and then there'll be no interruptions while I assemble the ingredients for my potion*.

'I, um, think I'll just go for a . . . an, uh . . . swim,' the Nose mumbles, backing out of the kitchen. 'Erm . . . when's supper?'

'Give me a couple of hours,' the Toad says, turning her back on the Nose in an attempt to hide the huge grin sweeping across her face. 'I'm cooking up something really, really special for tonight.'

Twelve:

Total toddler meltdown

Through the open door I can see that Mum and Dad have arranged buckets and pails all over Jack's bedroom floor. Outside it's still raining and inside it's still leaking, and there's a terrific din of plinks and plonks and splishes and sploshes as drips fall from Jack's ceiling into the buckets. Tomorrow a team of roofers will arrive and try to fix our leaky roof, but for tonight, Jack will have to carry on camping in

Daisy's room and Daisy in mine. When we came home from school, Jack moved a mountain of furry toys out of Daisy's room and into mine because he said he couldn't concentrate on his homework with all those goggly eyes staring at him. Great. With the arrival of a ton of teddies, plus Daisy and WayWoof, and Daisy's bed and all her picture books, my bedroom feels as if it's shrunk to half its normal size. Daisy may be the smallest person in our house but she seems to take up the most space. Tonight she ate the most supper as well. Somehow she managed to cram in three helpings of apple and raspberry crumble before Mum decided she'd had enough and hauled her off for a bath.

Daisy's already in bed with WayWoof asleep at her feet when I go upstairs to change into my pee-jays.

'What doon, Lil-Lil?' she demands as I

dump a herd of teddies off my bed and onto the carpet.

'Trying to get into my bed,' I mutter, turning my back on her while I take my clothes off.

'Oooooo,' she cackles, standing up in bed to get a better view. 'Bumbum, Lilybum, Daisybum—'

'DAISY!' I roar. 'Be-HAVE. You're really embarrassing me.'

'Not hayve. Not embassing you.'

'Yes you are.' I turn round and fling a teddy at her – at least, I fling it at where Daisy was half a second ago.

She's not there any more. The teddy sails across the space where my little sister was standing and bounces off the wall before falling onto Daisy's empty bed. WayWoof whimpers in her sleep and turns over.

'Daisy?' I'm dragging on my pyjama bottoms, wondering if she's hiding behind the curtains or if I'm going to have to go out in the cold and rain to find her.

I pull back the curtains. Nope. No Daisy.

Under the bed? Not there either.

In the cupboard? Not a sign.

Oh, for heaven's sake. Where is she?

Downstairs I hear Dad saying, 'I'll just go up and empty all the buckets, then I'll go and say goodnight to Lily and Daisy,' then there's the steady thump-thump of his footsteps climbing the stairs.

Aaaargh. Dad mustn't find out that Daisy's not here. I turn out the light and grab a pillow and stuff it along with an armful of teddies under Daisy's quilt. I'm hoping it looks like the hummock a sleeping toddler might make. It doesn't really, but I don't have time to make it any more realistic. I leap across the room just as the bedroom door starts to open.

'Dad. SHHHHHHH,' I hiss, standing in the doorway in front of him, rubbing my eyes as if I can barely stay awake. 'Whatever you do, Dad, don't wake Daisy. I've only just managed to get her off to sleep.'

Dad nods and mouths *OK*. He gives me a hug and heads off into Jack's bedroom to start emptying buckets.

Phew. For a minute there, I was almost positive he'd say, *What's that thundering sound, Lily? Is that your heart? Why is it hammering in your chest? Why are your*

eyes like saucers? Heavens, Lily – are you all right? Here, let me turn on the light and have a better look. Oh. OHHH.

And then – *Where is Daisy? Why is there a pillow and ten teddies in the middle of her bed? What's going on? Lily? LILY?*

So, yes. Phew and phew again. In Jack's room next door I can hear Dad sploshing and splashing and walking back and forth to the bathroom with brimming buckets full of rainwater. Finally he heads back downstairs. I look at my watch. It's half past nine. Where on earth is Daisy? Downstairs I can hear Mum talking to Dad and the distant murmur of the TV. These are the normal sounds of our night-time house; the sounds that send me off to sleep every night. Not tonight, though. Tonight I'm going to have to stay awake and wait for Daisy to reappear from wherever she's gone. I've decided there's absolutely no point in trying to find her; she could be anywhere. Even if I knew where she'd gone, I'd still be unable to find her. Witch Babies can turn themselves into anything they want, so it would be like trying to find a needle in a haystack. All I can do is wait . . . and wait . . . and wait . . . until Daisy finally decides to come home.

Daisy is nothing like as far away as Lily imagines. In fact, she is downstairs in the kitchen with her mum and dad, although not in a form that her mum and dad would recognize or celebrate. It is fortunate that Daisy's parents aren't aware that their youngest child has turned herself into a bluebottle. Bzzzzzz, **hwuuarglp**, goes Daisy. Her parents would be horrified if they could see what Daisy is doing to the remains of the apple and raspberry crumble. Eughhhhh. Don't ask. Bluebottles have the most revolting table manners. Once Daisy has eaten* her fill, she flies up to the ceiling and amuses herself for a while by walking upside down round the lampshade.

Unsurprisingly, her mum and dad don't notice a thing. They're too busy talking. Listen:

'If it keeps on pouring, I'll have to get up in the middle of the night and empty those buckets all over again,' Dad says.

BZZZZzzzzzzztzzzzTTT, Daisy buzzes, annoyed because one of the amazing sucker feet that enable her to walk upside down across the

* I use the word 'eaten' in the loosest sense. 'Eat' implies putting something into your mouth and giving it a good chew before swallowing it. Bluebottles don't really eat, they . . . No. *Eughhhhhhh*. I can't tell you. It's simply too horrible for words. Ask your mother to explain.

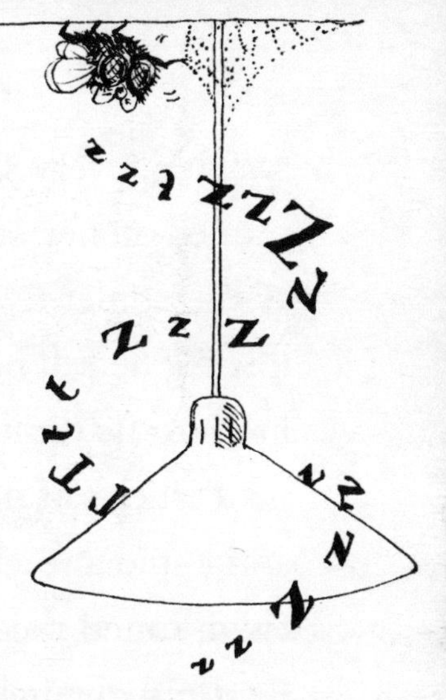

ceiling has become entangled in sticky spider's web.

'I'll do it,' Mum says. 'I'll have to get up in the wee small hours anyway, to change our baby girl's gruesome nappy.'

ZZZZZZt-ZZzzzzt-ZT-ZT Ztzzz, Daisy squawks, thrashing around in an attempt to disentangle herself from the web. To her alarm, she is becoming more and more trapped, not less.

'If only we could find some way to convince Daisy that nappies are horrible,' Dad sighs.

ZZZZZZrrghAAArgzzzzzz, Daisy yells, having discovered that there are many things that are even more horrible than nappies. One of these things is bearing down on her, its spider-jaws slavering and its hairy body swaying, every single one of its many eyeballs trained on her. In a panic, Daisy hauls and tugs at the spider's web in a last-ditch attempt to unstick herself before this monster spider turns her into its dinner.

Particles of dust drift down from the ceiling as the spider reaches out to grab Daisy in a lethal eight-legged hug. There's a frantic BZZZT, a crunch, then silence. Daisy has changed herself into the one creature she knows can be relied upon to swallow spiders.*

Fortunately, Daisy's mum and dad don't look up at this point, because there's a baby bird gliding down

* Songs learned at nursery school can come in very useful, especially if you happen to be a Witch Baby. They can, on occasion, save your life. Daisy has cause to thank Miss McPhee for teaching her the words to 'There Was an Old Woman Who Swallowed a Fly' - especially the bit when 'the old woman swallowed a bird to catch the spider that wriggled and squiggled and tickled inside her'.

from the kitchen ceiling; a baby bird that lands on the laundry basket, preens its feathers, does a quick poo, then drifts down to the floor, waddles across to the kitchen door and heads upstairs.

'Where have you been?' I whisper as Daisy finally toddles into our bedroom at twenty to midnight.

'Not a been,' Daisy mutters scornfully, falling face-down on her bed and adding, 'Go seep, Lil-Lil.'

'Daisy' – I try to make my voice as stern as possible – 'you can't keep on sneaking out at night like this. You're far too small to be out on your own. For heaven's sake – Mum and Dad would go bananas if they knew what you'd been up to. Promise me you won't do this again?'

There's a long silence. I'm hoping that this is

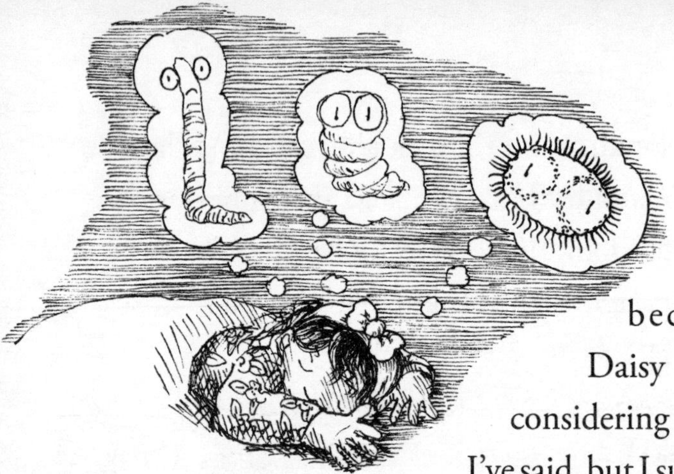

because Daisy is considering what I've said, but I suspect she's merely wondering what to turn me into next. A worm? A maggot? A germ?

'Come on, Daze. It's really late,' I groan. 'You should have been asleep hours ago.'

More silence. I'm just beginning to think she has fallen asleep, the wee toad, when there's a loud prrrat-a-tat-tat from her nappy. Uh-oh. Incoming poo. Time to go. The bog beckons. 'RIGHT. Let's go.' I leap to my feet and pluck Daisy off her bed. I'm halfway to the bathroom with her in my arms when Daisy launches into her best ever impersonation of a shriek alarm.

'NO WANTIT GO POTTY,' she bawls. 'NOOoOo. GO 'WAAYYYY. NO POO 'N LOO. NOT DUNNA POO. NO WANTIT NAPPY, NO WANTIT BUM BUM BUM BWAAAAAA . . .'

CRIKEY.

Lights go on all over the house as the MacRae family rush to the rescue of their youngest member. In seconds, we're surrounded. Daisy's roars of protest were loud enough to alert even Jack to her plight: he stands in the bathroom doorway, towel round his middle, hair full of shampoo suds and, for once, no earbuds jammed in his ears.

'Jeez, Daze. You're LOUD,' he says. 'For a minute there I thought you were the fire alarm.'

'NO WANTIT FILEARM,' Daisy shrieks. 'NO WANTIT—'

'Daisy' – Mum hauls her out of my arms – 'Lily is only trying to help—'

'NO WANTIT HELP,' Daisy wails. 'NO WANTIT BAFFROOM. NOT DUNNA POO. NO WANTIT NAPPY. NO WAAAAAAA . . .'

Mum and Dad communicate by waggling their eyebrows at each other as Daisy goes into a total toddler meltdown. When she pauses to draw breath, Mum sighs. 'Oh, darling. My poor Daisy. Poor little bunny.'*

For once, Daisy doesn't argue that she's notta

* Bunny? Bunny? My little sister? I cannot believe what I'm hearing. I've never met anyone less like a bunny than Daisy. She's a baby witch, for heaven's sake. Poor little troll, yes. Poor little Komodo dragon, yes. Poor little bunny? No way.

bunny. She gives a couple of shuddering, *hiccuppy* SObS and collapses against Mum's shoulder. In goes her thumb, her eyes roll shut, and in seconds she is fast asleep.

The sudden silence is deafening. How did she do that? One second she's a baby shriek alarm, the next, she's out cold . . . Dad goes into my bedroom and pulls back the quilt, then Mum tucks her in. There. It's that simple.

'I think we need to forget all about toilet-training for a while,' Dad says. 'Poor wee Daisy's finding it all a bit much.'

'I agree,' Mum says, standing up and stretching. 'Actually, I'm finding it all a bit much. I hate having to keep on nagging her, the poor wee sausage. She must think that we spend every waking moment worrying about the contents of her nappy.'

At this, Jack rolls his eyes and jams his earbuds back into his ears. I imagine that, like me, he tries *not* to worry about the contents of Daisy's nappy. *Urrrrghhhh.* I'm so glad I can't remember being small. Some things, like nappies, are best forgotten . . .

We're all standing round the sleeping Daisy, yawning our heads off, when WayWoof suddenly joins in with a forty-fang yawn, followed by a stretch, and then she rolls over and goes back to sleep. I may be the only member of our family* who can see her do this, but two seconds later we can all smell her. *Eughhhhh.* WayWoof – that is disGUSting. Mum's nose wrinkles, Dad coughs and Jack backs out of the bedroom, fanning his hand in front of his face.

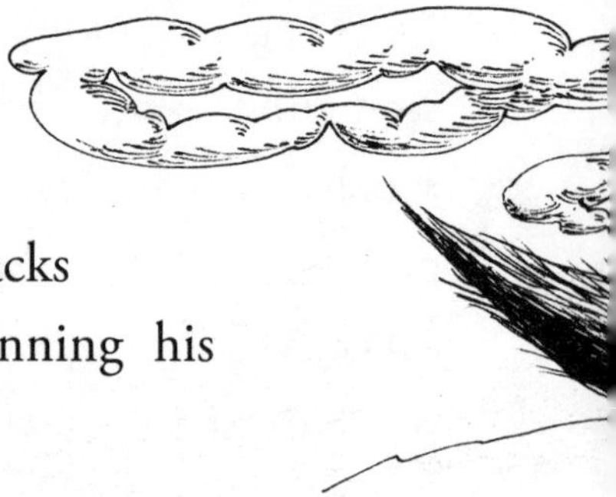

* Apart from Daisy.

Unsurprisingly, Mum and Dad assume the smell belongs to something Daisy has just laid in her nappy.

'**Yeeeurgh**, Daisy,' Dad whispers, shaking his head.

'Don't wake her,' Mum whispers back. 'I'll change her in the morning. **Phwoarrrrr**.'

I keep quiet. So does **WayWoof**. There are some things that Mum and Dad simply don't need to know about.

Thirteen:

A technical hitch

In her puddle-bed in the attic bathroom of Arkon House, the Toad is horribly wide awake. The soothing patter of rain on the roof failed to send her to sleep, as did the mug of cocoa before bedtime. Now it's half past three in the morning and the poor wakeful Toad suspects she won't get a wink of sleep. Her golden eyeballs feel like they've been rolled in sand, her legs like they've been filled with lead, but her brain is still buzzing around inside her head like a wasp trapped in a jam jar.

The same image is playing in her memory over and over and over again:

The Nose is sipping coffee from the wrong cup. She is raising the Chin's cup to her lips, and before the Toad can stop her, she takes one sip, smacks her lips, takes another sip, then another . . . then she swallows the whole lot in one greedy *gulp*. The Nose has just drunk the love potion intended for the Chin. This is a disaster.

The Toad blinks, trying to clear this unwelcome vision from her sight, but the vision refuses to go. The vision rewinds itself back to the beginning and doggedly starts again.

There is the Nose, reaching out to ladle five spoonfuls of sugar into her cup. There is the Nose tipping a thick dollop of cream into her cup. There is the Nose grating a lump of

chocolate into her cup. There is the Nose giving her cup a good stir. And there is the Toad, transfixed with **HORROR** as she suddenly realizes that the Nose has the wrong cup. The wrong cup? The cup meant for the Chin. The cup with the incredibly potent love potion smeared all round its interior. **Aaaaaaaargh**, the Toad thinks, but it's too late. Briefly she considers jumping onto the table and snatching the cup out of the Nose's hands, but it's too late for heroics. The Nose is taking a sip from the cup. The Nose smacks her lips and takes another sip . . . and another . . .

One sip was all it took. After all, as the Toad knew better than anyone, it was an incredibly powerful love potion which had taken hours to make. Sadly there's none left. One sip, followed by another, followed by a huge *gulp*, and that was the end of the potion. For the fortieth time that night the Toad puts her head in her hands and gives a deep groan.

'My plan . . .' she whimpers. 'It's ruined. Now the Chin will never fall in love with Mr Harukashi. Now there'll never be a wedding. Now I'll never, NEVER get to be a bridesmaid . . .'

From along the corridor comes the sound of a **cracked** and terrible voice attempting to sing a song.

'**Aiii lurrrrve a lah-dee,**' it wails. '**Ahhh baw-neeee heeee-lunn lah-dee.**'

The voice is ghastly; it sounds as if its owner's tonsils are made from a rusting sheet of corrugated iron across which someone is dragging a garden rake. The voice belongs to the Nose; every piercing squeak and shriek, each *honk* and **YELP** comes tumbling from her mouth while she serenades her reflection in the mirror of her dressing table.

'The towWWW-urrr of LURRRVE,' the voice continues. 'Ai-ai-ai-ai'm sohhh in LURRRVE with EWWWwWE.'

The Toad leans her head against the cool porcelain of the bath and groans some more. What a disaster. Since the moment when the love potion disappeared down the Nose's throat, the Toad felt as if she'd stumbled into a bad dream. Someone else's bad dream.

Within seconds of swallowing the potion, the Nose changed. One moment she'd been a nasty, sneery, poisonous old baggage; the next, she'd been transformed into a giggly, bubbly, gushy old madwoman who hugged and kissed everything within reach. Usually as silent and brooding as an approaching thunderstorm, the Nose started babbling and shrieking with laughter, clapping her hands and hooting as if she'd just heard the world's funniest joke. The Toad and the Chin sat in stunned silence as their sister rocked and jiggled and wheezed and slapped the tabletop, generally behaving as if her pants were full of ants and her brain had been replaced by a whoopee cushion. Tears of mirth rolled down her face as she staggered across to hug the fridge; gales of laughter erupted from her as she dropped a kiss on the dishwasher.

When she galloped out of the kitchen trailing a flurry of air-kisses, the Chin turned to the Toad and said, 'How much did she have to drink with her supper?'

The Toad blushed. She couldn't possibly tell the truth, but lying didn't come naturally.

'Er . . . um, ah . . . yerrrsss . . . no . . . why d'you ask?'

'WHY DO I ASK?' the Chin bawled. 'Because she's acting as if she's DRUNK! She's falling about, hugging the furniture and – listen. Is that her singing?'

From upstairs came the Nose's terrible voice raised in song:

'When aiiiii forrrrl in LURRRRVE . . .'

The Chin **shuddered**. '**Ssso undignified**,' she muttered. 'She's making a complete fool of herself. So embarrassing. I can't bear to listen. She's not acting like herself at all. The **Sisters** of HiSS never behave like that.'

Hysterical giggles drifted down to the kitchen as the love potion continued to dissolve four hundred years of nastiness. The Chin squinched up her face as if she'd bitten into a lemon. Draining her coffee cup (*The wrong cup*, thought the Toad miserably), she stalked across the kitchen to the bread bin and opened the lid.

'You can't *still* be hungry?' squawked the Toad. The three Sisters had just worked their way through a three-course dinner, ending with a chocolate raspberry meringue cake of such deliciousness that both the Nose and the Chin had devoured three helpings. Each. Hence the Toad's shock at seeing her Sister raiding the bread-bin. Her confusion deepened as the Chin took out a loaf of bread, cut herself a slice, removed the crusts and tore the slice in two

before stuffing one half in each ear.

'Whatever are you doing?' the Toad demanded.

'I CAN'T HEAR YOU,' the Chin roared in

reply. 'WHICH MEANS I WON'T BE ABLE TO HEAR THE NOSE EITHER.' And with this, she stamped out of the kitchen; moments later, her bedroom door slammed shut.

Whoops and yells of delight continued to echo down the corridors of Arkon House as the Toad loaded the dishwasher, wiped the table, took out the rubbish, swept the floor and blew out the candles. Wearily she clambered upstairs

and into her bedroom, closing the door behind her. The sound of tinkling laughter coming from the Nose's room was followed by a muffled thumping sound as the infuriated Chin banged on the wall separating her from her *giggly* Sister.

'Shut up!' she shrieked. 'SHUT UP! SHUDDUP! I can still hear you even with half a loaf stuffed in my ears.'

'Ooh, ooh, ooh, I DOOOO LURRRRRVE yoooOo,' the Nose sang.

In desperation, the Toad climbed into her bath, tore the bath sponge in two, stuffed one piece in each ear and sank beneath the water. **Ahhhhhh.** There. Peace at last.

Sometimes being an amphibian had its advantages.

Outside the window, rain continued falling, pouring down the roof, rolling along gutters and gushing down drainpipes. Across the morth-west of Scotland, rivers rose, low-lying fields flooded and huge puddles turned into proper lakes.* By the time a grey and drizzly dawn arrived, the weather had become front-page news.

* Known locally as lochs. As in: *Och, yon puddle's turned into a right loch.*

Fourteen:

A near miss

If Monday was wet, yesterday was a complete washout, but at least when we finally arrived at school we *were* able to splash our way across the playground. However, today the water was so deep there that we had to use the back door to get into school. Despite all the rain, the whole school is buzzing with excitement. Our school concert is the day after tomorrow, or as I said to Daisy, only two more sleeps to go.

'Two seeps?' she said, holding out four fingers.

'Two,' I replied, curling two of her fingers back into her palm and patting the remaining two.

'Ony two?' she whispered, obviously hardly able to believe that the concert is so close. 'Two seeps and Daisy's a munk.'

For some reason she won't say 'monkey', preferring to call herself a 'cheekmunk'. Fortunately I can understand what she means, even if nobody else can.

'Ooooh,' she breathed. 'Go packtiss song now.' And off she toddled, leaving me to hang up her coat and hat and scarf and put her wellies in the row of wet shoes by the radiator.

Today is the dress rehearsal. Mrs McDonald and Miss McPhee are getting the nursery children ready while we older ones put out the scenery and arrange chairs in the hall. To my relief, the ceiling has stopped dripping, which is rather odd because, if anything, the rain has become heavier. However, there is a rather ominous dark stain on the ceiling;

yesterday, when I first noticed it, it looked like a rabbit, but today it's more like a vast octopus.

'Gonny stop staring into space and give me a hand here, Lily?' Craig gasps, trying to drag one of the bits of scenery across the hall. 'I can't do it on ma own.'

Between us, we haul the huge canvas across the floor.

Through the open nursery door I can see Daisy waving at me as Miss McPhee fits the monkey mask onto her head. Vivaldi is helping Annabel lay out the blue silk across the stage, and Jamie and Shane are arranging rows of chairs for the audience to sit on. Yoshito is helping Mr Fox, the school janitor, test the microphones when, all of a sudden, there's a FZZzzZZBzzzZZT sound and all the lights go out.

Since it's only eleven o'clock in the morning, we're not plunged into darkness, but along with the lights, the microphones have stopped working. Mr Fox frowns: when things go on the blink, it's his job to try and fix them, but before he can do anything, there's a **CRaaAAACK** followed by a colossal CRUMP, and a massive chunk of the ceiling falls down with a loud **CRASHHHH**!

'QUICK!' Mr Fox yells, grabbing Yoshito and pushing the emergency fire doors open.

'Everybody outside. NOW.'

Across the hall I can see all the little ones in their costumes, crowding behind Miss McPhee. Mrs McDonald is comforting several wailing tots as she leads them outside, carefully avoiding the enormous pile of broken plaster and bits of ceiling lying in the middle of the hall. *Gulp*. Craig and I were incredibly lucky not to have been standing under the ceiling when it fell down. If we hadn't been dragging the scenery up to the stage at that precise moment, we would have been directly under that pile of plaster.

We all herd outside into our drowned playground. Water laps around our feet, and by now most of the nursery children have picked up on the general mood and are wailing. This is the **PITS**. I'm freezing cold and my feet are wet, but the worst thing is that I've just overheard Mrs McDonald saying to Miss McPhee, 'What a shame. I'm so sorry, but this probably means we won't be able to have our concert on Friday.

The poor wee mites are going to be so disappointed.'

No concert? After all our hard work? That's so unfair. I may not be a poor wee mite but I am so disappointed, I want to scream out loud. Vivaldi splashes across to stand beside me, followed by Annabel. They both look thoroughly miserable.

'This is just completely rubbish,' Vivaldi hisses, wrapping her arms around herself and shivering. She doesn't know just how rubbish it is, because she didn't hear what I heard.

I tell her: 'Did you hear? Mrs McDonald said we won't be able to have the concert this Friday after all.'

'WHAAAT?' Annabel squawks. 'No concert? But . . . but . . . but we *have* to have the concert.'

'No withoot a roof, we don't,' Craig says

grimly. 'Think aboot it. We can't ask people to come to the concert and make them sit under umbrellas, can we?'

'This is just **PANTS**,' Shane says, frowning mightily. 'Rubbish weather. Ah hate rain. When I'm big, I'm no gonny live in Scotland any more. I'm gonny move somewhere it doesn't rain, like the desert or something.'

'That's just stupid,' Craig tells him. 'You can't live in the desert. There's nothing in them except sand.'

'And no rain,' Shane snaps. 'Besides, ah like sand. Sand's OK by me. And anyway, there's loads of stuff out there in the desert. Like . . . pyramids. I've seen them on TV.'

'What're you on aboot?' Craig snorts. 'Are you gonny live in a pyramid, then?'

'AYE,' Shane yells. 'That's fine by me too. I'll wrap myself in bandages like a mummy.

Anything rather than stand here getting wet.'

After a moment's thought Craig says smugly, 'You can't live in a pyramid and I'll tell you why.'

'Why no?'

'Because there's nowhere to plug in your PlayStation,' Craig tells him – but before Shane can come up with a convincing argument, Mrs McDonald calls us all over.

'Children. Listen carefully, dears. We're now all going to go back into the nursery classroom. Miss McPhee is phoning your parents to get them to come and take you home. I'm afraid we're going to have to close the school.'

A huge '**AWWWWWWW!**' goes up. A few of the littlies promptly sit down in the puddles.

'Mrs McDonald? Does this mean that there will not be a concert on Friday?' Yoshito's face looks utterly woebegone.

'I'm afraid not, dear. There's nowhere else big enough to hold all of us and the mums and dads. I'm very sorry, but we're going to have to postpone our concert until later in the year.'

By now, all the nursery children are crying. This is rapidly turning into the worst day ever. We all troop back into the school and crowd into Daisy's classroom. To make matters worse, most of the littlies are still wearing the costumes we made for them to wear at the concert, and they are soaking wet, so we have to help take them off and drape them over the radiators to dry out.

'We may as well just dump everything in the bin,' Craig mutters, peeling the elephant mask off a sobbing tot. 'It's no as if we're ever gonny use any of the costumes.'

For once Annabel is silent. She stands there, biting her bottom lip and staring out at the rain.

Beside her, a tiny child dressed as an ant drips watery black paint all over the floor.

'I've managed to get hold of all the mums and dads,' Miss McPhee says, 'except Jamie and Annabel's.'

'Typical,' groans Jamie. 'Today's the nanny's day off and Dad will probably be at work till late afternoon.'

'Come back to my house,' I suggest, pulling the monkey costume off Daisy. 'You can tell him to come and get you once he's back.'

'Poor munk,' Daisy says, her voice muffled by her furry monkey mask. 'Notta cheekmunk now. Munk all wet.'

She's right. The monkey costume is soaking. Clumps of brown fur are coming off in my hands. **Eughhh**. I look like a werewolf.

'Are you sure?' Jamie asks. 'I mean, that's awfully decent of you. There are two of us, you know.'

'I'm sure Mum won't mind,' I lie, suddenly remembering the mess with the roof, the state of Jack's room, and the builders, who'll be trooping up and down the stairs. And it won't just be Jamie coming over for tea: Annabel will be coming too. Crikey. If Mum ever speaks to me again, it'll be a miracle.

Mum blinks a bit when she discovers that she's been given two extra children to look after, but then she rises to the occasion heroically.

'Brilliant,' she says. 'I was wondering how Lily and I were going to manage to move all Jack's stuff into the study. Thank heavens you're here, Jamie and Annabel. I don't know how we would have managed without you.'

They *are* helpful too. Without so much as a *squeak* of protest, they carry box after box of Jack's things into the study. Occasionally

Annabel
looks thoughtful
and Jamie asks lots of
questions.

'Why has your brother got a fur coat?' Jamie is half buried under this item.

'It used to belong to our grandfather,' I explain. 'He travelled around Russia a lot.'

'Oooooh. Was he a spy?' Annabel asks.

'No, he was a piper actually. He toured with a pipe band all over the world.'

'Is that why you play the pipes?' Jamie asks.

'No . . . well . . . sort of,' I mumble, remembering the tune I've been practising for months specially for the concert. The concert which, as of today, has been cancelled. Suddenly I feel really miserable.

Almost as if she can read my mind, Annabel says, 'You were going to play a tune at the concert, weren't you?'

I nod, not trusting myself to speak in case I burst into tears of disappointment.

'I'm so fed up,' Annabel says. 'I was really looking forward to doing my sea-thing with all that blue silk . . . Now we'll never know how good it might have been.'

At which point Mum calls us downstairs for supper.

Fifteen:

Sister for sale

Daisy's already in her high chair, swigging from her cup with loud slurping sounds. WayWoof is curled up invisibly under the table, waiting for whatever falls off Daisy's plate. Dad is back from work early and Jack is slumped in his seat, staring into space with his earbuds tsss-tsssing as usual. Mum has squeezed two more chairs round the table for our guests and the kitchen is full of delicious smells. Mum starts dishing out spaghetti into bowls and passing them round. Daisy takes one look at hers and gives a wail of dismay.

'Notta wumz,' she moans. 'No likeit WUMZZ.'

We all grit our teeth. Daisy always maintains that spaghetti is worms, but with a bit of persuasion she can usually be talked into eating them. I'm sure she doesn't really believe they're worms; she's just a complete Drama Queen.

'WUMZZz,' she bawls, locking eyes with Annabel. ''GUSTING.'

Oh, dear. At Mishnish Castle I bet Jamie and Annabel are used to eating dinner from antique porcelain plates on linen tablecloths, without horrible baby sisters comparing their food to nasty squirmy things.

'Here, havva WUM,' Daisy *cackles*, digging her fists into her bowl and extending a dripping handful.

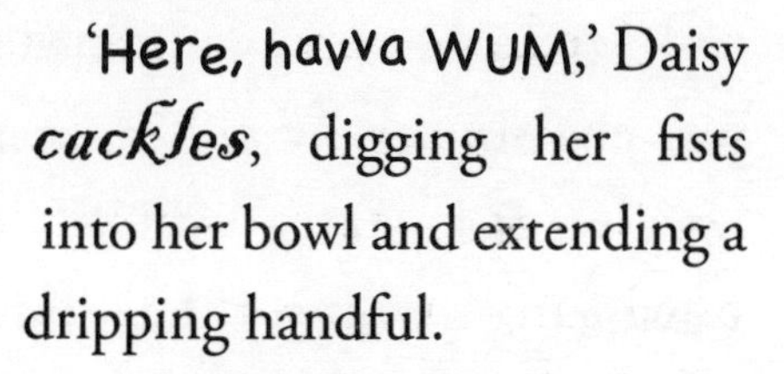

'DAISY,' Mum snaps. 'Stop that. I'm so sorry,' she continues, turning to Annabel. 'She's in one of her wicked moods today. Not enough sleep last night, and now, with the concert being cancelled at your poor school . . .'

'I think she's really sweet,' Annabel says. 'I wish *I* had a little sister . . .'

My jaw falls open and I stare at Annabel, but before I can say anything, Jack gets in first.

'Have ours.' He grins. 'Really. We wouldn't mind, would we, Daze?'

Daisy rakes him with one of her why-don't-you-just-shrivel-up-and-die stares, then focuses on Annabel. 'Havva WUM,' she commands, waving a wriggly handful in Annabel's direction.

'Delighted,' Annabel replies, pretending to eat some. 'Yum. Delicious. Got any more?'

Oh, no. I've just spotted what Daisy's done. **Yeeeeeurgh**. Those are actual worms. Annabel

can't see that Daisy is playing for real. Oh, gag. Oh, how horrible is that? Poor Annabel. I have to stop her from eating any more.

'DAISY!' I roar. 'Not funny. Not funny at all. Stop it or—'

'Not lissnin', Lil-Lil,' Daisy says. 'La-la-la. WUMZ. La-la-la—'

'Daisy,' I hiss in her ear, 'if you don't stop this right now, I won't read you a bedtime story.'

'Not lissnin'. No wantit story. Go WAY,' Daisy shrieks.

'Tell you what, Annabel,' Jack says. 'We'll pay you to take her. What d'you reckon? A hundred pounds?'

'Better make that two,' Dad says, smiling at Daisy. 'She's really expensive to run.'

'Three,' Mum says. 'She costs a fortune in nappies.'

'NOT THREE,' Daisy bawls, flinging her handful of worms across the table. Fortunately I'm the only one who can see

them *wriggling*
and thrashing
next to the salad bowl.
Everyone else thinks it's just a pile of squished spaghetti.

'NOT THREE,' Daisy repeats, banging her fists on the table. 'Not lissnin'. Not FUNNY. Not WAAAAAAAA . . .'

At which point Dad plucks her out of her high chair and takes her upstairs for a bath. Phew. Silence descends on the kitchen.

'I'd better see if I can get hold of Dad,' Jamie says. 'He should be home by now . . .' He excuses himself and goes out into the hall to use the phone.

Annabel and I clear the table and Mum dishes out pudding. Yum – she's made an upside-down lemon and apple sponge, and there's vanilla ice cream to go with it.

Annabel's eyes light up. 'Wow,' she says. 'Can I come and live with you, Lily? We never have dessert at home.'

'I'm sure you do, really,' Mum says, giving Annabel an extra-big helping.

'No,' Annabel says sadly. 'Absolutely not – unless Dad's having a dinner party or something, and then there are loads of desserts but we're not allowed any till the next day.'

Golly. There'd be a riot here at the Old Station House if we weren't allowed pudding till

the day after. What's the point of that? Puddings are meant to be eaten straight from the oven. Talking of which . . .

We're just scraping the last atoms of ice cream out of our bowls when Jamie returns. He looks really uncomfortable, as if he's trying to hide how upset he is.

'Um . . . bit of a problem, Mrs MacRae. Er, Dad's got his dates mixed up and it turns out he's in Barcelona tonight and can't get back home until . . . er . . . tomorrow.'

'Tomorrow?' squeaks Annabel. 'But . . . but . . . who's going to look after us?'

'Er, yes,' Jamie continues, his ears turning pink with embarrassment. 'And I phoned Katinka . . .' He turns to Mum and explains, 'Our nanny. But it's her day off and she's not answering her phone and—'

'Don't worry,' Mum interrupts, patting Jamie's arm and smiling reassuringly at Annabel. 'Really, Jamie. These things happen. You'll both stay with us tonight, OK? Let me have your dad's phone number and I'll let him know you're safe and will be spending the night with us.'

Jamie's shoulders slump with relief. Hoorah for Mum. All of a sudden I'm so proud of her, I want to stand up and cheer.

Annabel bites her lip and asks, 'D'you think I could speak to Daddy after you?'

'Of course,' Mum says. 'I'll only be a couple of minutes. Help yourselves to pudding while I phone.' And off she goes to ring Mr Dunlop, the Absent Dad.

Moments later, it's Annabel's turn. Poor her. It must be pretty weird having a dad who forgets he's supposed to be looking after you and your big brother. If that had been our dad, I would have been feeling pretty cross and upset too.

Mum sits down at the table and groans. 'I forgot. Of course. Tomorrow there won't be any school, will there? Oh heavens. Never mind – you'll all have to stay here with me and the roofers . . .'

Annabel returns, eyes shining and practically bouncing back to the table. 'Great news,' she says. 'You'll be terribly impressed. Guess what

– I've managed to get Daddy to allow us to have the school concert at Mishnish Castle. Isn't that BRILLIANT?'

At first I can't believe what I'm hearing. The concert is on again? Just like that? How on earth . . . ?

'I made Daddy feel really, really bad' – Annabel grins – 'since he'd managed to forget all about Jamie and me. I mean, that was pretty shocking, really. I told him we'd already been having the most awful day with the school ceiling falling down and were all feeling completely miserable about the concert being cancelled. I didn't really have to say much more. Well . . . maybe just a couple of *hiccuppy* sobs . . .'

Jamie rolls his eyes and groans. Jack is gazing at Annabel in utter **HORROR** – he'd no idea girls did that sort of thing.

'It was Daddy's idea,' Annabel said finally. 'Well . . . sort of.'

Wow. I *am* impressed. I'm also feeling a huge bubble of excitement rising up in my chest. *YESSSSSS! The concert is going to go ahead. The show will go on, thanks to Annabel.* Then, all of a sudden, I'm panicking. **Aaaaargh**. The costumes. The scenery. The music. Will there be time to do it all before Friday? Only two more days to get ready.

'Can I use the phone?' I ask. I can't wait to tell Vivaldi.

Sixteen:

A near miss, Hiss

Unable to sleep, the Chin was sitting alone in the kitchen at Arkon House, trying to read the latest issue of *Hexenkessel: the monthly magazine for Real Witches.*

In vain she tried to concentrate on Euphemia Nightshade's column on 'Goblins I Have Known

and Eaten', but her heart wasn't in it. Turning to Zorba's Horrorscopes, she began to read that instead. Next to her star sign (the Wilted Nettle) she found the following:

> *This month the stars are shining just for you, helping you make an ENORMOUSLY important decision.*
> *Lucky word: Yes*
> *Lucky stone: Diamond*

The Chin blinked in surprise. Usually her Horrorscope was full of doom and gloom, not to mention **boils**, **warts** and *plagues*. And her lucky stone was, more often than not, a lump of coal. She blinked and read once more – *Lucky stone: Diamond*. The Chin frowned, then snorted with disbelief. Where on earth was she supposed to find a diamond to be lucky with? What a load of old tosh. Zorba the Horrorscope writer must have washed his brains out with bubble bath.

Flinging the magazine into the bin, the Chin was about to head upstairs to attempt to get some sleep when the telephone began to ring. Who on earth could be calling at this hour? It was only half past five in the morning. It was still dark, for spawn's sake.

'Hello?' she **croaked**, picking up the receiver.

'Mischin?' whispered the voice on the other end; then, not waiting for a reply, it carried on rapidly, the words tumbling out breathlessly, one after another without pause: 'It is I, Hare Harukashi, your neighbour. And friend. And sincerest admirer. Yes. So. Oh, Mischin, how to say this? I find myself unable to think properly, Mischin. My thoughts are running around in

circles like a flock of badly behaved sheeps—'

'Sheep,' the Chin corrected, but Hare wasn't listening.

'. . . and I, who once could sleep for days on end, cannot find so much as a moment's slumber—'

'Nor I, Mr Harukashi,' the Chin confessed. 'Not one wink of sleep last night—'

'Dear lady,' Hare interrupted, 'I have to ask

you a question. You must think very hard before you answer because . . . well, I cannot explain why, but I know that if I do not ask you this question, I will never sleep ever again.'

'Dear me,' the Chin murmured. 'How very dramatic, Mr Harukashi. Very well. I'm listening. Fire away.'

There was a silence on the other end of the phone, and then Hare gave a sigh so deep, it appeared to have come from underground.

'No, Miss Chin. I cannot ask this question down the end of a telephone. It is too important. I must see you, I must look you on the face when I ask you.'

'**Erm . . . um . . .**' the Chin faltered. Whatever was the matter with this man? 'Well, if you think that's really necessary, then by all means ask me when we next meet.'

'NO!' Hare yelped, unable to stop himself.

'I cannot wait that long. Dearest lady, even a day feels like an eternity—'

The Chin stood up, then sat down again. She was curiously unsettled by this peculiar conversation. Hare, normally such a mild-mannered human, was behaving as if he'd swallowed an electric eel. What on earth was going on?

'I need to see you at once,' he went on, his voice dropping abruptly to a whisper. 'Right away. Well . . . as soon as I take Yoshi to her friend's house . . . and she is coming down for breakfast now, so I must go. Say ten past nine? Please say yes? Please?'

What was a witch to do? The Chin rolled her eyes and agreed, but as she replaced the receiver, it dawned on her that she had no idea what she had just agreed to.

Good as his word, Hare knocks at the door of Arkon House at exactly ten minutes past nine.

'Knock, knock, knock on the door of LURRRRVE,' yodels the Nose, practically flattening the Toad in her haste to answer the door. To the Toad's horror, it is Hare Harukashi on the doorstep, face to face with the Nose, who has undergone an overnight transformation into a *giggly fluff*-brain.

'Oh, helurrrrrrrr,' the Nose purrs, a huge smile breaking out across her face. 'You delightful little fellow. And heavens, what a handsome suit you're wearing. And a flower in your buttonhole too, you cheeky little chappie – why, you look as if you're going to a wedding.'

Behind the Nose, the Toad has her head in her hands and is rocking back and forth, making small *whimpering* sounds of dismay. Across the hall, the Chin is struggling into her coat and counting to ten in an attempt to stop herself from turning the Nose into a louse. *How dare she!* she thinks. *Hare has come to see ME, not to be dribbled all over by her.* Jealousy, an unfamiliar emotion, flares in the Chin's heart. *He's mine*, she thinks. *All mine.*

'Ooooh, come in, come in, doooo,' coos the Nose, plucking at Mr Harukashi's sleeve and trying to drag him inside. 'A cup of tea? Coffee? Champagne?'

'Oh, for SPAWN'S SAKE,' says the Chin. 'Would you SHUT UP for once? One: we don't have any champagne, two—'

'*Two for tea and tea for two*,' the Nose sings. '*You for me and MEEEE for YOOOOOU.*'

'TWO,' bawls the Chin, 'Mr Harukashi has come to see me about something very important. And THREE—'

'Three?' the Nose bleats, batting her eyelashes.

'Three's a crowd,' the Chin snaps

triumphantly, snatching Hare's other arm and propelling him backwards. 'So we're going OUT.' And with a slam of the door, they're gone.

*

An hour later, the Chin returns alone. In the kitchen, the Nose is sulking by the fire and the Toad is baking cakes.

'Change of plan,' the Chin says, pouring herself a cup of tea with an unsteady hand. 'The school concert is to be held at Mishnish Castle instead of the school.'

The Toad stops stirring and peers at her. 'Was that the reason Mr Harukashi came round earlier?' she asks.

'Just to tell us that? Couldn't he have phoned instead?'

'Mmmmmh?' the Chin mumbles, turning away to hide the sudden blush that is setting her face alight. She is still reeling from what Mr Harukashi has said; not the bit about the change of plan for the concert, but the bit when he got down on his knees in a puddle and asked her to—

'Are you all right?' the Toad says, gliding into view in front of her.

'YES!' squeaks the Chin. 'Fine. I'm fine. Never better. Why d'you ask?'

'Your face is like a beetroot,' the Toad remarks; then, realizing that this probably wasn't the most tactful thing to say, 'I mean, your face is all, er, red. Rosy red. You look like a rose.'

'*MY LURRRRRRVE is LIKE a red, red ROSE*,' the Nose sings, glaring into the fireplace and adding, 'How selfish you are, Chin. Keeping that lovely little Mr Harukashi all to yourself. Mother always said that we should share.'

'*Mother?*' gasped the Chin. 'Mother was a grumpy old troll who never shared so much as a cold with us.'

'Well, I still think we ought to share everything,' the Nose mutters. 'Starting with Mr Harukashi. Bags I get to sit beside him at the concert.'

'Never mind, Chin,' the Toad says, trying to make peace. 'I'll sit next to you, so you won't be on your own.'

'Whatever are you talking about, Toad?' the Nose says. 'Read my glossy blush-pink lipsticked lips. You. Aren't. Going. To. The. Concert.'

At this, the Toad gulps, puts down her

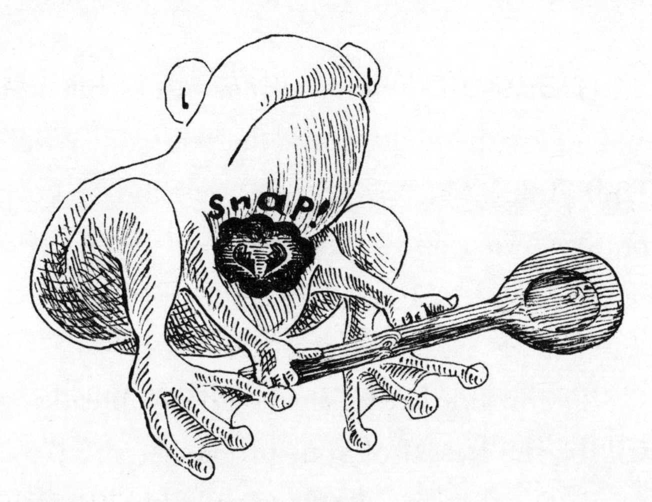

wooden spoon, and gulps again. Her eyes fill with tears and she takes a deep breath. Inside her, something goes **SNAP!** 'YOU,' she bawls. 'YOU, NOSE, ARE THE MOST FOUL, SELFISH, GRABBY, UGLY, MEAN OLD WITCH THAT EVER LIVED.'

'Thank you,' the Nose says happily. 'I do try my best to be vile.'

'I WISH I HADN'T WASTED A PERFECTLY GOOD LOVE POTION ON A TROLL LIKE YOU!' the Toad shrieks in fury.

OOOOPS. The Nose springs out of her seat and grabs the Toad round her throat. 'What. Did. You. SSsSSay?' she demands. 'Love potion? What do you mean?'

'I . . . I . . . I . . . I . . .' the Toad wheezes. 'I . . . ca . . . n't . . . brea . . . the.'

'By the time I've finished with you, breathing will be the leassst of your problems,' the Nose **hisses**, tightening her grip. 'What did you mean *love potion*? Are you telling me that you sneaked a love potion into my tea?'

'**N-n-n** . . .' the Toad gasps, aware that if she tells the truth, the Nose will probably tear her limb from limb. Then inspiration strikes. '**NO!** I didn't just give you *one* love potion, I gave you seven. Seven super-strength, shaken-not-stirred potions, each one guaranteed to turn even the most **WICKED** witch into a little *puff* of *fluffy* loving-kindness.' She heaves a theatrical sigh, chokes back a sob and continues, 'But you, Nose, you are without a doubt the strongest and most powerful witch ever to draw breath. My seven love potions simply bounced off you. They didn't change so much as a hair on your head. You're still as foul and **WICKED** as ever.'

At this, a strange expression crosses the Nose's face. Instead of looking furious or insulted at the Toad's attempt to change her nature, she looks decidedly smug. Smirking to herself, she places the Toad on the table and peers at her.

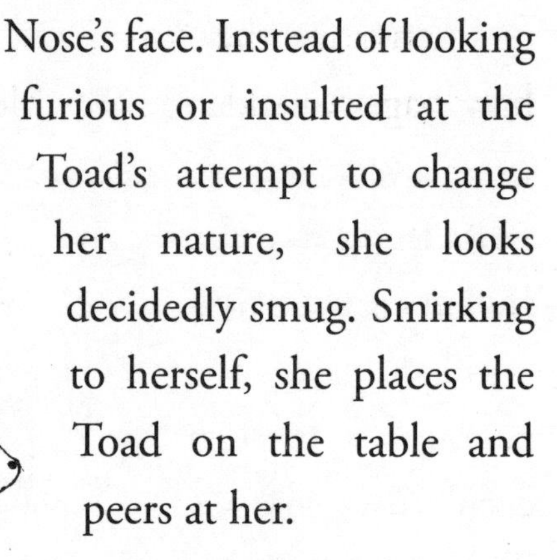

'Hmmmm,' she says. 'Well . . . you *failed*, Toad. You failed to change **MEEEEE**, wonderful and **WICKED MEEEEE**, potion-resistant **MEEEEE**. You silly old *fluff*-brained fool of a failed frog – d'you know what? I feel so sorry for you I've decided you can come to the concert after all.'

The Toad blinks. What fresh hell is this?

'Yerrrrrs,' the Nose says. 'You can go as a handbag. An old one. An old bag. *Teee-heeee-heeeee*. You won't even have to dress up.' And with this final insult, she **stamps** out of the kitchen and heads for the pool.

Seventeen:

Tonight's the night

A line of car headlights stitch through the twilight towards Mishnish Castle. Our audience is arriving. Tonight is the night of the school concert. Aaaaargh. Watching all the cars coming towards us is making me feel so nervous I think I'm going to be sick. Except Mishnish Castle is so huge, I probably wouldn't be able to find a bathroom to be sick in. Ever since we got here we've all managed to get lost at least once, our cries of 'Where am I?' echoing along corridors and staircases, because the castle is even bigger inside than out.

We're all busy dressing the nursery children in their costumes. They look brilliant, parading up and down excitedly in front of an enormous

mirror, then playing Hide-and-Seek behind the curtains. We're getting ready in a first-floor bedroom which is bigger than our school hall, and when it's time for the concert to begin, we'll all walk very slowly down the main staircase into the huge hall where our audience will be waiting.

'Wid you look at that statue!' Craig elbows Shane in the ribs, his face turning brick-red with embarrassment.

'That's no decent. He hasnae got any pants on.'

'That's nothing,' Shane whispers. 'There's a

picture in the bathroom with a psSWhsss and she's Whssspsss with a big shhhpsSs.'

Craig and Shane burst out laughing, but I'm not really paying any attention to them because I'm watching all the mums and dads arriving outside. Grandparents have been invited as well – Yoshito's dad is helping two old ladies to clamber out of his car, and Mum and Dad have promised to bring Granny and Grandpa MacRae. *Gulp*. This makes me feel even more nervous, since it's Grandpa's bagpipes I'm going to be playing in roughly half an hour.

AAAAAAAARRRRRRRRGH.

Things I'd rather be doing tonight than playing my pipes:

a) Singlehandedly defending Planet Earth

from an alien invasion, armed with nothing more dangerous than a blunt spoon (that's me with the spoon, not the aliens).

b) Eating a bowlful of the nursery tadpoles. Raw. Without salt or pepper.

c) Climbing Ben Screeeiiighe in a pair of buttered flip-flops.

d) Grooming Annabel's grumpy* pony, Polka, with a broken-handled toothbrush.

'Lily?' Vivaldi's piercing whisper drags me back to the present. 'Look at the dogs.'

I drag my gaze away from the drive, where my entire family are gazing up at the hugeness of Mishnish Castle with their mouths open. Behind Vivaldi, Jamie and Annabel's ancient black dog, Petra, is running round and round the furniture, leaping over chairs, crashing into tables, skidding into nursery tots and generally acting like a mad puppy. Considering Petra has spent the last ten years of her doggy life snoozing by the fire or s . . . l . . . o . . . w . . . l . . . y waddling upstairs to collapse on Jamie's bed, tonight's sudden burst of speed is remarkable.

* Polka has already bitten Craig, and if Shane hadn't been so quick to react, he would have launched him into orbit with a well-aimed kick. The best word to describe Polka is 'foul'.

'PETRA!' Jamie roars. 'COOL THE BEANS, WHAT?'

'Oh, good LORD,' Annabel *yelps*, leaping across the room to catch a toppling lamp. 'Calm down, dog.'

'Whatever has got into her?' Jamie makes a lunge for her, but fails to grab hold of her collar. 'SIT!' he roars, but Petra ignores him completely, running out of range, dancing around in circles and barking madly.

'I've never seen her like this before,'

Annabel says, sounding puzzled. 'It's as if she's seen a ghost or . . .'

Or a **Waywoof** perhaps? Daisy's invisible dog is running in circles around poor Petra and winding the old dog up like a clockwork toy. Petra can see WayWoof, as can Daisy, Vivaldi and I, but nobody else can.

'DAISY?' I yell, and across the room, a small monkey looks up.

Daisy is busy getting her furry leggings pinned on.

'WHAT WANTIN' NOWWWW, LIL-LIL?' she yells back.

I can't yell

at her to call WayWoof off, so I point at the orbiting dogs and *waggle* my eyebrows. Fortunately Daisy gets my message, and to my relief, WayWoof stops mid-circuit and trots obediently over to her side. **Phew**. Petra immediately stops cavorting around and slumps down onto the floor, exhausted.

'Right, Lily dear,' Mrs McDonald says. 'It's time.'

Downstairs, a clock begins to chime. Oh, help. Surely it's not seven o'clock already? My stomach flips and I feel cold all over. OH, AAAARGH. It's time for the concert to begin. Beside me, Vivaldi takes her guitar out of its case and softly plucks a chord.

Oh, lucky her.

One thing you can't do with a set of bagpipes is softly play anything. Softly? Bagpipes don't do soft. I lift the lid, and there they are, collapsed in a little heap, the drones sticking out like giraffe legs. Lying in their case, they look almost pathetic, like a big, flat, tartan balloon. As I reach out for them, I remember that bagpipes were instruments of war. Bagpipers used to lead the Scottish clans into battle. The Highland chieftains didn't send in the cannons or the archers to soften up the enemy. They sent in the pipers. Cleverly, they chose to stun the enemy with **LOUD** music. They knew that after five minutes of being forced to listen to **DEAFENING** reels and strathspeys, the enemy would agree to anything. *Take our lands, our castles, our sheep, our cows, our treasures – even our women and children, they would beg.*

Take anything you want, but please, turn . . . the . . . volume . . . DOWN.

I blow air into the bag, tucking it under my arm and slinging the drones over my shoulder. All of a sudden I feel good. I'm ready. Between my elbow and my ribs, my pipes are swelling like a sail. They're ready. Across the room, Miss McPhee has the littlies all lined up. They're ready. Mrs McDonald opens the door to the hall, and downstairs, our audience has fallen silent. Everything is ready.

I take a deep breath. Let's begin.

The MacRae family find themselves behind Mr Harukashi and his guests. Jack is sitting behind an old lady with a big nose who is balancing a vast lumpy handbag on her lap. Being Jack, he doesn't notice when the handbag blinks. Mum is behind Hare Harukashi and Dad is behind a

woman with long silvery hair who is sitting so still, she might be a statue. Granny and Grandpa MacRae have turned right round in their seats and are looking behind them. This is because they don't want to miss a single note of their grand-daughter's pipe playing. They are staring at the top of the grand staircase, waiting for Lily to appear.

Everyone else is looking at the scenery: Craig's looming black clouds against Yoshito's bruise-coloured sky. Back in the school hall, the bits of scenery looked enormous, but here in Mishnish Castle they are dwarfed by the high ceilings and vast staircases. In fact, the scenery looks a bit lost, propped up against the far end of the hall. There's no stage here, no curtains to *swish* open or shut at the beginning and end of the concert. However, Mr Fox and Mr Dunlop, Jamie and Annabel's dad, have worked wonders with lights and speakers and microphones, and they are both sitting at the back of the hall behind a table full of controls and remotes and switches, ready for the concert to begin.

The grandfather clock begins to chime the hour. *One, two, three . . . eleven, twelve, thirteen* . . . Mr Dunlop shrugs and shakes his head. Finally the clock stops chiming at nineteen o'clock. Marvellous. Time to begin. The audience falls silent.

Eighteen:

Lucky word: Yes

Upstairs, a door opens. There's a second's pause and then the audience hears a sound as old as Mishnish Castle itself. Wilder than the wind and a hundred times louder, it's the sound of Lily MacRae leading her entire school downstairs into an evening to remember. As the sound of the pipes *skirls* and swoops around Mishnish Castle, windows shake, chandeliers tinkle and car alarms go off outside on the driveway.

Tears spring into Grandpa MacRae's eyes. He is so proud of Lily he thinks he might be about to explode.

Tears spring into Mr Dunlop's eyes too. In a downstairs alcove, he's just seen his priceless P'ing vase explode into a thousand pieces. Bagpipes are **LOUD**.

Tears also spring into Mr Harukashi's eyes, for his beloved Mischin has just whispered, 'Yes,' in his ear.

Yes, she would love to.

Yes, she has finally realized that life without Hare and Yoshito would be no life at all. Being a witch is all very well, but you can't hug a cauldron, and broomsticks never bring you breakfast in bed.

Yes, she wishes to be a Miss no longer. To be Mrs Harukashi Mk 2 would be an honour.

Yes, from *fairy godmother* to Oddmother, the Chin is delighted to accept Hare and Yoshito's proposal of marriage.

*

'YESSSSSSS!' *yelps* the Toad, practically falling off the Nose's lap in amazement at this unexpected turn of events. 'RESULT!'

Disguised as a handbag, she's been eavesdropping on the conversation between Mr Harukashi and her sister, so she knows exactly what the Chin has just said 'yes' to. **YESSSSSSS!** There will be a wedding at last, she thinks, tears not only springing into her eyes, but springing out too, gushing over the Nose's lap and making her knees all wet.

As Lily marches through the audience,

followed by the rest of the school, the Nose leans down and mutters into her handbag, 'What are you hissing at, Toad?'

And before the Toad can stop herself, she blurts out the Chin's marvellous news.

'I'm so HAPPY!' she squeaks. 'The Chin is going to marry dear Mr Harukarrrghhhhhhh—'

But she doesn't get to finish whatever she was about to say, because now the Toad is tumbling end over end, falling to the floor. Towering above her, the Nose has stood up – and she's furious, she's **RAGING**, she's so incandescently angry that sparks are shooting out of her mouth, her eyes, her ears, her nostrils and, I am sorry to say, her bottom.

She is so infuriated that for a moment she is on the verge of throwing a **Compleat Wobblie**, which would turn the entire west coast of Scotland into a melted pile of volcanic ash. Her feet stamp on the floor, nearly skewering the poor Toad on the end of one of her vicious high heels. She looks exactly like a toddler having a particularly bad tantrum, and all around her, heads are turning to glare and make *shhhhh*ing sounds. Who is this horrible rude old lady who is interrupting the concert? Before the Chin or the Toad can shut their sister up, Grandpa MacRae steps in. Grandpa MacRae used to be a pipe major – which, as everyone knows, is no job for the faint-hearted.

'Would you sit DOON, lassie,' he hisses in a penetrating whisper. 'I canny see a thing for all your FUSSING.'

And miraculously, the Nose does as she is told. However, the expression on her face is volcanic. On the floor at her feet, the Toad is frantically undoing the spell that turned her into a handbag. Handbags aren't much use when your Sister is about to explode. The Toad knows from experience that the Nose may be sitting down and behaving herself right now, but she is secretly stoking her RAGE, fanning the flames of fury until the time is right for her to erupt again.

At the other end of the hall, oblivious to all this drama, Lily has finished playing and the audience roars its approval. Pink with relief and embarrassment, she bows and steps to one side. Now it's Yoshito's turn. She looks tiny, standing up there at the front, hands clasped round a microphone, dressed in pyjamas as if

she's going to bed. Her eyes roam across the audience until she finds first her father, then her *fairy godmother*, Mischin. All at once, Yoshito's eyes widen and her face lights up with happiness. Mischin has nodded 'yes'. Eyes shining, Yoshito hold the microphone up to her mouth and sings,

'It's raining, it's pouring,

the weather's really boring.
I'd rather be in bed instead
of getting up in the morning.'

Then, shuffling and smiling shyly, the nursery children line up on either side of her, sit down on the floor and pretend to be going to bed as they join in with the song:

'It's raining, it's pouring,
we're in our beds and snoring.
We'd rather stay in bed instead
of getting up in the morning.'

Nineteen:

Playing for keeps

This is *brilliant*. Now that I've played my first tune, I can actually start to enjoy myself. Everyone's laughing at all the right bits and I think it's going really well. Sitting facing us in the front row, Mrs McDonald and Miss McPhee are smiling happily, nodding their approval at the nursery children and occasionally herding them back into their positions at the front. Then the first song is over and Yoshito steps aside to tumultuous applause and cries of 'MORE, MORE, BRAVO!'

While the audience are working themselves up into a frenzy, Craig and Shane pull a huge bit of brown scenery up to the front. This was supposed to be the ark, but it got wet when the

roof leaked and all the colours ran into each other, and ever since, Craig has called it the Big Jobby. He might have a point. Annabel and Jamie run across in front of the ark with their long strips of blue silk, getting them ready. Mr Dunlop is walking along the hall lighting candles, one by one, until there are hundreds of tiny points of light flickering all around us. From the back, Mr Fox gives Vivaldi the thumbs-up, and she steps forward, pale as a ghost but determined to do her best. Mr Fox turns out the lights, and all of a sudden the scene is set. Jamie and Annabel begin to waft the long strips of silk up and down like waves on the sea . . . Wow. What a magical effect. It looks just like the sea . . . It's brilliant. We're off in the ark, with Vivaldi playing the first chords of the song we could all sing with our eyes shut.

'The animals went in two by two –
Hurrah, hurrah!
The animals went in two by two –
Hurrah, hurrah!
The animals went in two by two,
the elephant and the kangaroo,
and they all went into the ark
for to get out of the rain.'

Amazingly, Daisy seems to be singing the proper words, not the awful poo-version which drove poor Miss McPhee to despair. I am delighted to see that she's behaving really well, and not like a little WITCH at all. For some reason **WayWoof** hasn't left her side since we all came downstairs. It's almost as if she's guarding Daisy – but from

rrrrrrrrrrr

what? I can't see anything dangerous or threatening, but **WayWoof**'s fur is standing up on end as if she's seen something she doesn't like.

Maybe it's Mr Dunlop's hideous collection of deer antlers that's upsetting her. **Ugh**. Poor deer. I don't know how Jamie and Annabel can sleep at night in a house with all these bits of dead creatures stuck to the walls. Maybe that's why Daisy is so quiet and well-behaved too . . . either that, or she's done a poo and is hoping that if she keeps quiet, nobody'll find out. I'm watching her really closely, but I can't tell what's going on in her little witchy head. She's in the middle of the nursery children, her little face glowing in the candlelight, singing merrily,

'The animals went in five by five,
by hugging each other they stayed alive,
and they all went into the ark
for to get out of the rain.'

And now . . . it's time for her to step forward and do her little act. I cross my fingers. Let's hope she doesn't blow it now. *Please, Daisy*, I beg silently. *Please be a good monkey?*

'The animals went in six by six –
Hurrah, hurrah!
The animals went in six by six –
Hurrah, hurrah!
The animals went in six by six,
they turned out the monkey
because of its tricks,
and they all went into the ark
for to get out of the rain.'

Daisy is running around madly, pulling terrible faces, *waggling* her tongue, *wiggling* her bottom and making loud OO, ooh, OOO, ooh noises. Fortunately, this is exactly what she's supposed to be doing – until the elephant and the kangaroo step forward, take her by the arms and push her away from the ark. *Ahhhhh. Poor monkey.* There's a huge round of applause for Daisy, then she runs through the audience and off towards the back of the hall, where it's too dark for me to see her any more. *Well done, Daisy. That was perfect.* She'll sit with Mr Fox for a bit; then she'll come back up to the front and join in with the very last verse.

Now it's the turn of the tot dressed as a little pink pig, and she stumbles up to the front to stand blinking out at the audience. Behind her, the nursery children **shuffle** and clear their throats in readiness for another verse. All of a sudden there's a small *flurry* of activity in the audience as somebody stands up and walks out.

I can't quite make out who it was – it's too dark to see. Maybe they don't like pigs.

'The animals went in seven by seven –
Hurrah, hurrah!
The animals went in seven by seven –
Hurrah, hurrah!
The animals went in seven by seven,
the little pig thought it had gone
to heaven . . .'

The sound of singing fades into the distance as **Witch Baby** runs along the corridors of Mishnish Castle with **WayWoof** at her heels and the Toad following closely behind. Witch Baby is looking for a bathroom, WayWoof is looking out for Witch Baby, and the Toad is just hoping she'll be in time to stop anything dreadful happening. The Toad has a hunch that something awful is coming their way. For once, the Toad is absolutely right.

Some way behind, a dark shadow flits from wall to wall; the shadow of a woman with a very big nose and an even bigger temper. Moonlight streams through a window, and the Nose is briefly illuminated as if, like the children downstairs, she is onstage. But this is no children's play about arks and floods and animals; the Nose's face is too scary for that. The way the Nose looks now, she'd give the nursery children NIGHTMARES for a month.

Sadly, the love potion has completely worn off and the Nose has turned back into herself: a grumpy, mean and vicious old WITCH. Forced to watch the children's concert and listen to the Toad *wiffling* on about the Chin's wedding, the Nose realized that her sisters had completely lost the plot. What were they thinking of? Children? Concerts? Happy songs? Weddings? The Chin and the Toad were no longer fit to be called Hisses. She herself – the Nose – was the only true Sisters of Hiss.

It was at this exact moment that the Nose decided that it was time to go back to Ben Screeeiiighe. Time to go back to being a proper WITCH, without her silly soft sisters; back to lonely, windswept Ben Screeeiiighe all on her own . . .

And it was at that precise moment that Daisy, in her monkey costume, ran past.

Suddenly the Nose saw that she didn't have to go back to Ben Screeeiiighe on her own.

Moments later, crouched in the shadows, she sees Witch Baby and her ridiculous dog shriek to a stop outside a bathroom door, and she realizes it's time. The tot is near-as-makes-no-difference toilet-trained. So . . . *Tonight's the night*, thinks the Nose. *Tonight I collect our Witch Baby*. No matter what nonsense her Sisters had spouted about waiting for the sun to be in the correct sign, or the moon to be in the proper phase or whatever – none of these things matter because the Nose has decided that NOW is the time. She's fed up with waiting. She's sick of living surrounded by rude and stupid humans. She is going to go home to her lonely house on top of Ben Screeeiiighe, and she's going to take **Witch Baby** with her, no matter what anyone says.

Twenty:

Monkey business

Witch Baby is unaware that she's being watched. All she can think about is how much she needs to go to the bathroom. For once, she doesn't want to fill her nappy. Perhaps it's something to do with being a monkey. Witch Baby has the sneaking suspicion that proper monkeys don't wear nappies, and she does so want to be a proper cheekmunk, even if only for this one night . . .

Ahead of her is a door. She pushes it open – and yes, it's a bathroom. Moonlight spills through the window, so Witch Baby can clearly see the toilet, looming up ahead. She can't see the Toad, high up above, clinging to the cistern and peering down at her with big golden eyes. Now for the tricky bit. She begins to wrestle with her monkey costume, but the tail keeps getting in the way, and her furry leggings are held up with safety pins . . . Aaaargh! What's a Witch Baby to do?

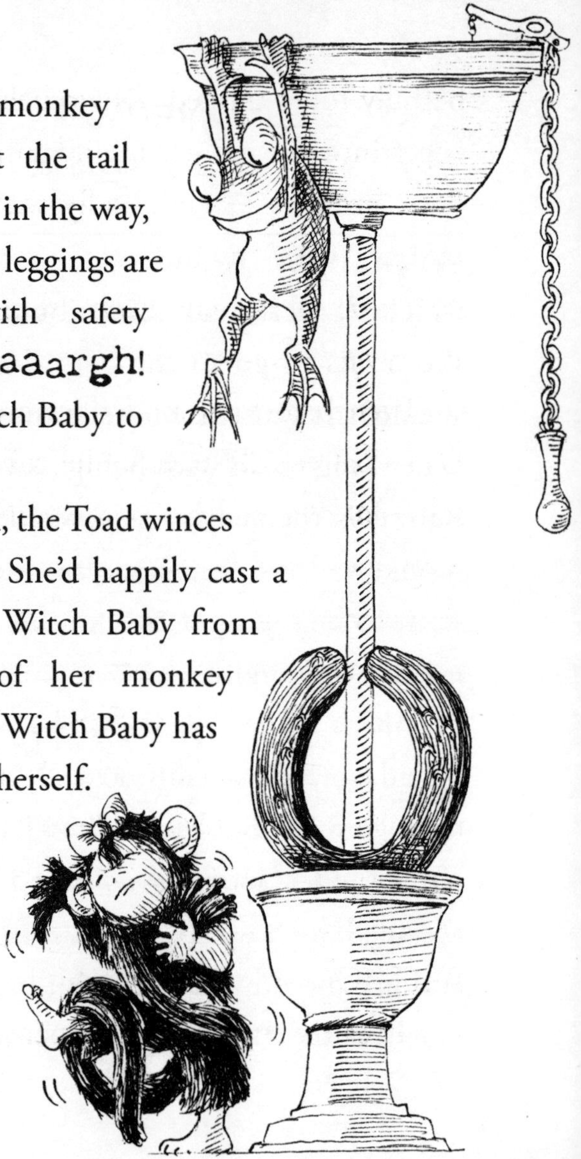

Overhead, the Toad winces in sympathy. She'd happily cast a spell to free Witch Baby from the bonds of her monkey costume, but Witch Baby has to learn for herself. That way, she'll grow up to be a great witch, PLUS she'll be fully toilet-trained. Down below, WayWoof edges into the bathroom and turns to face the door, growling meaningfully with her hackles raised.

Hurry up, Witch Baby, the Toad thinks. *Hurry up before—*

Even before the door flies open, knocking Daisy backwards against the toilet, WayWoof starts **barking** madly – for there, in the doorway, with her hands outstretched to grab Daisy, stands the Nose.

'**Preciousssssss**,' she hisses, '**I've come to take you back home to Ben SSSSSCreeeiiighe**.'

Daisy blinks. Whatever is this old lady talking about? Daisy doesn't want to go home right now. 'Go way, WITS,' she mutters, adding by way of explanation, 'NEEDA BAFFROOM.'

'It can wait,' the Nose snaps, 'but I can't.

Come on. Let's go, kid.'

'NEED A POO,' Daisy says crossly. 'GO 'WAY, WITS.'

But the Nose isn't listening. She's flexing her fingers and pumping her single eyebrow up and down. Up in the cistern, the Toad stifles a *squeak* of terror. She knows the signs: all that finger-flexing and eyebrow-waggling means that the Nose is about to throw a spell. Uh-oh, thinks the Toad. *Please don't let it be a Compleat Wobblie. Anything but that . . .*

The Toad will never find out exactly which spell the Nose had in mind because suddenly WayWoof lunges forward and sinks her teeth into the Nose's leg. Had the Nose been human, she wouldn't have felt a thing, but because she's a witch, she screams, 'YOWWWWWWWWCH – GERRROFFF, YOU BRUTE,' and all of a sudden WayWoof flies across the bathroom and smacks into the wall with a thud. **Ouch**. Poor WayWoof. The Nose kicked her. Had the Nose been human, her leg would have passed straight through WayWoof, with neither of them feeling anything, but because she's a witch, WayWoof **yowls** in pain. **Uh-oh**. That does it. Daisy steps forwards and hits the Nose in the tummy.

'NOT hurtit, WayWoof. BAAAAD WITS,'

she yells. 'GO 'WAAAAY.'

'DON'T YOU DARE HIT ME, YOU FOUL BRAT,' the Nose yells back.

'NOTTA FOUL BAT, YOU A FOUL BAT,' Daisy insists, holding her hands up and twiddling her fingers.

There's a squawk, a hiss, and then the Nose *shudders*, shivers – and turns into a huge bat. It flaps about madly, trying to wrap its massive black wings around Daisy. She *struggles* and *wriggles*, but she's no match

for this monster. Over by the wall, WayWoof *staggers* to her feet and tries to bite the bat, but it flies out of reach, dragging Daisy behind it.

'NOTTA BAT – YOU A CAT!' Daisy yells, and the bat *shudders* and falls to the floor, sprouts four legs and a tail, then promptly tries to sink its claws into her leg. WayWoof goes **crazy**, biting and snapping at the cat, but it fights back, hissing and *snarling* until Daisy is afraid that WayWoof will be hurt.

'STOPPIT!' she shrieks. 'BAAAD PUSSYCAT. STOPPIT. BAAAD PUSS – notty, notty, notty.'

The cat doesn't appear to care how naughty Daisy thinks it is. It ignores Daisy completely, and creeps closer to WayWoof, arching its back and shadow-boxing with all its claws extended. Watching from above, the Toad decides something has to be done before blood is spilled.

Hopping down from the cistern, she lands in between WayWoof and the cat, but Witch Baby gets there before her.

'YOU A BAD WITS,' she says, and the cat turns back into the real Nose. Uh-oh. The real Nose looks very, very cross indeed. Her hair is whipping around her head like a nest of snakes, and sparks are once more shooting out of her bottom. The Toad *quivers* with fear, WayWoof whimpers with terror, but Witch Baby is unstoppable. This time it's for keeps. This time the spell is non-reversible.

'YOU A BAAAAD WITS,' she begins. 'You hurted my WayWoof.'

'Oh, for fang's sake,' the Nose snaps. 'Would you get a grip, you stupid child. It's only a dog. Dogs aren't important, not like witches. Nobody cares about dogs. Now come on, we've wasted quite enough time already – it's time we were off to—'

'You a BAAAD wits,' Daisy says. 'No likeit BAAAAD witses. Poor WayWoof—'

'Oh, SHUT UP about that blooming dog, you vile little child,' the Nose **shrieks**, grabbing Daisy's arm and beginning to haul her towards the door. 'There are far more important things to think about than dogs. And don't even begin to think about taking – YIP – home to Ben Screeeiiighe with us. Dogs – YAP – a complete waste of space, and they don't even taste – WOOF. I can't abide – ARF. Nasty, hairy, dribbly things. YAP, YIP – foul – HOWWWWL – beasts with – WUFF WUFF. Hang on – what the YOWWWWWWWL?'

Where the Nose had been there now stands a

small and very ugly dog with a big nose. The Nose opens her mouth to growl, but all that comes out is a tiny YIP.

'GO 'WAAY HOME, baaad dog,' says Daisy.

At this, the Nose makes a half-hearted attempt to bite Daisy's leg, but when WayWoof growls at her, she turns tail and flees, yipping faintly, back down the corridor, out of the front door . . . and away.

Just like Daisy told her to, the Nose has gone home.

Twenty-one:

Daisy victorious

We are all lined up at the front, smiling and bowing as the audience clap and cheer and yell 'BRAVO!' The nursery children are pink with pleasure, Miss McPhee and Mrs McDonald are almost *glowing* with happiness, and as I look out into the audience, I can see that even Jack has taken his earbuds out. **WOW!** We *must* have been good.

Finally the applause dies away, Mr Fox turns all the

lights back on, and sadly, it's time to go home. We troop back upstairs to pack up our stuff and help the nursery children change out of their costumes. Daisy is so ridiculously over-excited I think she's going to burst. She's running around the room making monkey noises, tripping over everyone's bags, getting in the way and generally being a complete pest. Plus she's determined to tell the entire school all about her recent victory over the **FORCES OF DARKNESS**.

'Did a POO INNALOO,' she bawls at her best friend, Dugger. Poor Dugger turns white

and looks as if he's about to pass out. Even WayWoof gives a yelp of protest and lies down with her paws over her ears.

'Er, Daze . . . perhaps you might like to keep this amazing news to yourself?' I suggest, but Daisy is past caring what I think.

'NOT INNA NAPPY,' she explains in a voice like a foghorn. 'INNA LOO.' Then, just in case anyone is in any doubt about what she's on about, she adds, 'BIIIIG SPASHHHHH.'

Oh, dear. Time to go. Time to get my little sister home before she can say anything else. WayWoof stands up, stretches and then releases a small and powerful cloud of dog-gas. **Eughhhhh**. Great. Thanks, WayWoof. Quick, let's get out of here. I pat Daisy's arm and say, 'Come on, Squirt, let's go,' but Daisy has other ideas. Daisy is in one of those moods.

'Wozzat YOU, Lil-Lil?' she demands, flapping a hand in front of her face. 'PEE-YOO, Lil-Lil. You SMELL. DUNNA POO?'

'Shut up, Daisy,' I mutter, but she's on a roll. There's no stopping her.

'Wozzat YOU, Valdy?' she bawls, and even though it wasn't, Vivaldi turns pink. Time to go. I practically drag Daisy downstairs.

'Wozzat YOU, Dugger?'

'Wozzat YOU, Gamma?'

'Wozzat YOU, Gampa?"

Oh, the shame.

All the way home, Daisy plays this wonderful new game:

'Wozzat YOU, Dada?

'Wozzat YOU, Mumma?

'Wozzat YOU, Dack?

until we long to stop the car and *hurl* her into the bushes – 'Wozzat YOU, bushes? – but finally, two minutes from home, she falls fast asleep. It isn't until Mum and Dad peel her out of her monkey costume that we all discover that Daisy was telling the truth about the poo inna loo and the big spash. *HOORAH!* Her nappy is dry. There's no poo, no nothing in there. Daisy is now, officially, a proper human being.* Mum and Dad are so excited about this that you'd think Daisy had just flown to the moon and back.

* Not to mention a fully toilet-trained witch.

Jack and I leave the three of them in my room celebrating the Night of the Dry Nappy and head downstairs to make toast. Outside, for the first time in ages, the rain has stopped. It's so quiet we can hear a dog barking way off in the distance. Without all the rainclouds in the way, the sky is full of stars. Jack and I take our toast outside and look up at the night sky.

'What d'you reckon, Lil?' Jack mumbles through a mouthful of toast and peanut butter. 'D'you think there's anyone out there?'

'What?' I say. 'On a different planet?'

'Yeah. You know. I'm not talking about some sort of cheesy alien with an aerial sticking out of its head, or a man made of green cheese. I mean an alien that looks like us, but is completely different inside.'

I'm on the verge of blurting out, *What? D'you mean like Daisy?* but I stop myself just in time. Jack would never believe me if I told him. He'd think I was mad. Poor Jack. He probably thinks all babies are like **Witch Baby**.

'No,' I reply eventually, swallowing my last mouthful of toast. 'No. I'm pretty sure there's nobody out there, because if there was, we'd have seen them when they returned to pick you up and take

you back ho—' And I'm off, running across the garden, *whooping* and cackling like a Witch Baby Big Sister, pursued by my poor big brother, who still, despite being much older than Daisy and me, hasn't got a clue what's going on.

Ae last Hiss

You have to be unbelievably brave or foolhardy to make it to the summit of Ben Screeeiiighe. If by some lucky fluke you manage to avoid the gales that peel you off the ridge and hurl you like an old banana skin into the valley below, chances are, the treacherously icy path at the top will prove to be your undoing. Most mountaineers would rather suck soggy cornflakes off their crampons than attempt the summit of Ben Screeeiiighe. Most human mountaineers, that is.

However, mountaineers who used to be witches but have been permanently turned into small dogs . . . well, they're different. This might explain why, despite pouring rain,

hard sleet, driving snow, howling gales and an ice storm blowing straight out of the North Pole, there is a little dog with a big nose determinedly clawing its way up to the perilous peak of Ben Screeeiiighe. At times the dog disappears from sight as it tunnels through snowdrifts; at other times it nearly slithers off the edge of icy ridges, its **FROZEN** claws scrabbling for purchase on the slippy rocks. Finally, sides heaving with the effort, the dog reaches the door built into the top of the mountain and collapses in a heap on the doorstep.

Home. The Nose is home at last.

All she has to do now is open the door and crawl inside, out of the storm. But this is easier said than done. Push and **heave** as she might, she can barely open the door by more than a paw's width. She gives a *yelp* of disbelief. Is she to die out here in the storm, millimetres from safety? She pushes again, but the door remains obstinately stuck. What on earth is stopping the stupid thing from budging? The Nose **heaves** and *pants* and pushes against the door time and time again, but the door doesn't move.

GRRRRRRR, the Nose goes, furious at the stubborn door that refuses to open.

'WUFFF WOOOF, arf, yelp,' she barks, but the door stays where it is. She makes herself as small as possible and squeezes her muzzle into the gap between the door and its frame. Ah. In the dim light, she can just make out a vast pile of envelopes jammed behind the door. Nine whole months' worth of unopened mail for the Sisters of HiSS lie between the Nose and the shelter of home. The Nose's tail droops. *This isn't fair*, she thinks. If only she could use just a tiny little bit of magic to make the envelopes disappear . . . but it is a well-known fact that dogs can't do magic. Only witches can, and the Nose isn't a witch any more. Whatever the spell was that Witch Baby cast back in the bathroom at Mishnish Castle, it turned the Nose into a real, proper, no-nonsense, no-magical-anythings, one hundred per cent doggy dog.

'AWOOOoOOOO,' howls the Nose.

Since she fled from Mishnish Castle, she hasn't stopped running for two whole weeks. Two whole weeks? She's exhausted. All she wants to do is lie by a fire on a comfortable cushion and chew something tasty. Instead, she has to squeeze her paws under this stupid door and try to extract this stupid pile of post, one stupid, stupid, stupid letter at a time. For a split second she is so furious that she spins round and bites her own tail.

'OWWW,' she howls. 'ArooooOOOo.'

The wind answers back, louder and longer: WHOOOoOOOo WHOOOoOOOo oO-OO-oO.

The Nose gives a little whine. *Poor, poor,*

pitiful me, she whines. But the wind whips her fur and a flurry of snow stings her eyes. Brrrrrr. It's freezing up here on the top of Ben Screeeiiighe. If the Nose doesn't get a move on, she's going to turn to ice. *Better get on with it*, she thinks.

There's only enough room to remove one envelope at a time. The Nose tugs and scrapes and teases and claws nine months of junk mail, monthly editions of *WitchWit*, Cauldron & Kettle and The Goblin's Digest, two telephone directories (a few pages at a time), one office supplies catalogue (ditto), eighteen supplements to the office supplies catalogue, ninety-three begging letters, three tax returns, and countless envelopes with a variety of mis-spellings of the Toad and the Chin's names. Sadly there appear to be no interesting envelopes for the Nose. Not one. The Nose's tail droops lower and lower. It's just as she always suspected. Nobody loves her.

Then, with a *creak*, the door flies open and the Nose tumbles inside. There are only two

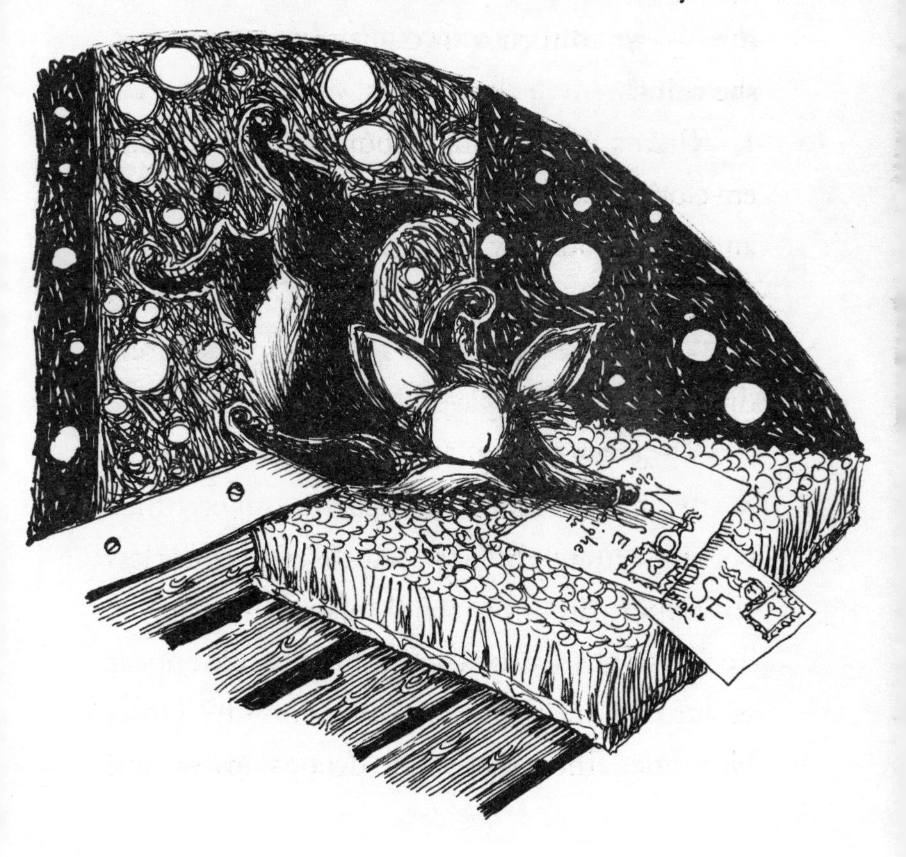

envelopes left on the doormat, and she almost flings them into the wind, unread. Almost, but not quite. Something about the envelopes catches her eye – she can't read, never has been able to, but she can recognize her own name when it's written down. That's easy-peasy. Her name is:

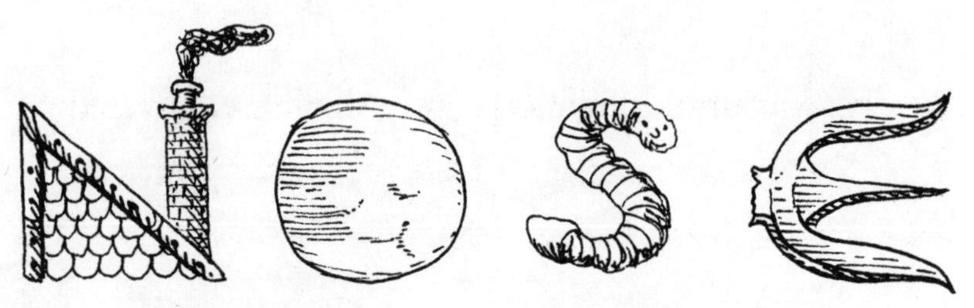

N – a roof with a big tall chimney; followed by

O – a moon; then

S – a wiggly worm; and finally,

E – a fork with its handle broken off.

N-O-S-E. The last two envelopes are for her!

Immediately her tail springs upright and begins to wag. She nearly turns round and bites it again, but stops herself just in time. Picking the envelopes up in her mouth, she trots into the house and nudges the door shut behind her. The wind dies to a far-away **shrieK**. There. **Phew**. Home at last.

It isn't until much later, after she has discovered that dogs are completely useless at lighting fires, cooking supper or doing anything other than being Man's Best Friend, that the Nose remembers her envelopes. Holding the first one in between her paws, she nibbles carefully round all four of its edges until the envelope falls apart

and what's inside tumbles out. It is a single card, made from thick creamy paper with a golden rim. The Nose sniffs. The card smells faintly of fish fingers and – she sniffs again – and chips. Not thick greasy chips, but thin ones cooked in olive oil. By now, the Nose is so hungry, she's *drooling*. Whiskers quivering with anticipation, she takes a big bite out of the card, but it doesn't taste of anything much. Her tail droops and she gives a ***yelp*** of disappointment. Peering at the half-chewed card, she can see her name written in the centre of it, but she cannot understand any of the squiggles written all round it.

The Nose cannot read. Poor Nose. She'll never know that she was invited by

Never mind. In fact, it's probably all for the best because the Nose might have made a nuisance of herself at the wedding – biting the bride, growling at the groom and doing all sorts of doggy things to embarrass the guests. Heaving a huge sigh, the Nose turns her attention to the other envelope, gnawing her way through it as she did before.

Several somethings fall out of this envelope: two photographs and one paper napkin-wrapped slice of cake. Being a dog, she falls upon the cake and gobbles it up in three seconds flat,

icing, marzipan, napkin and all. It isn't until she looks at the first photograph and sees the Chin and Mr Harukashi cutting an enormous, white-iced, three-tier wedding cake that the Nose realizes what she's just devoured.

Wedding cake? Her sister's wedding cake? Her sister married Mr Harukashi? The Nose gives a huge '**GRRRRROWFF**' of dismay. What kind of behaviour is that for a Sister of Hiss? Getting married? The very idea! In a blind rage, the Nose spins round and **SNAPS** at the first thing she can sink her teeth into, which happens to be her own tail. As her teeth close around it, it occurs to the Nose that biting one's own bottom isn't particularly good behaviour for a Hiss either.

Panting rapidly, she drops her tail and turns her attention to the second photograph. At first she has no idea why anyone would bother to take such a picture – it's of a huge tartan cushion in front of a blazing fire . . . with a bowl full of bone-shaped biscuits lying beside it. A bowl with N-O-S-E written on the side. Huh? And now the Nose is howling sadly: not only does her tail hurt from where she bit it, but the sight of that tartan cushion and the blazing fire – not to mention the bowl of dog biscuits – has made her feel so homesick that she wants to **HOWWWWWWL**.

So she does. Very loudly, but with a lot of feeling. She misses home so much it hurts. Even though she has just spent two weeks running all the way here to Ben Screeeiiighe, she now knows that Ben Screeeiiighe will never feel in the least bit like home. **No**. The Nose howls once again because she realizes that home is about people, not places. Home, the Nose realizes, is anywhere that the Toad and the Chin are. And this Sisterless house on top of Ben Screeeiiighe is no home at all. **AWoOOOOOOOo**.

Then the Nose realizes that all this howling and tail-biting is completely unnecessary. She doesn't have to stay on top of Ben Screeeiiighe in this cold and heartless home. She doesn't have to be lonely and unloved. She doesn't even have to be hungry . . .

The photograph is proof that she has a home. A real home. With a blazing fire, a tartan cushion and a bowl with her name on it. The photograph is a message from her family back home to tell her that she is loved, no matter what she has become. At this happy thought, the Nose's tail begins to wag uncontrollably.

And then it occurs to her that if she gets a move on and runs like the wind all the way back . . . she might just get home in time to share the last of the wedding cake.